FATAL
REUNION

by

CLAIRE McNAB

BELLA
BOOKS
2022

Bella Books, Inc.
P.O. Box 10543
Tallahassee, FL 32302

First published by Naiad Press 1989
First Bella Books Edition 2011
Second Bella Books Edition 2022

Edited by Katherine V. Forrest

ISBN 13: 978-1-59493-286-1

About the Author

Claire McNab lives with her life partner and a menagerie of two German Shepherds and two tortoise-shell cats in the beautiful northern beaches area of Sydney, Australia. She is the author of last year's best-selling *Lessons in Murder*, the first appearance of Detective Inspector Carol Ashton.

For Hoz

Acknowledgement

To Katherine V. Forrest is due deep appreciation and thanks for her incisive editorial guidance and for her warm encouragement.

Chapter 1

Everything was in slow motion. Each movement was choreographed.

He moved forward, loomed, threatened.

The threat was ending. The knife went in, up under his ribs—twisting under his ribs.

His face went slack. He said, "Please…"

The sound of his fall vibrated against the walls: sent ripples that went on, out into the world.

When the telephone rang Carol was laughing. She ruffled Sybil's red hair as she went to answer it. "Carol Ashton."

"Carol?"

In the pause, the heartbeat, Carol felt the room shift, become different.

"Carol, it's me—Christine."

After the slightest hesitation she said, "I know."

Of course she knew. It was a voice she would never be able to forget.

"Carol, I need you."

"Why?"

"It's Mitchell…he's dead. They think I killed him. Carol?"

I have a choice, thought Carol.

"All right," she said, "I'll come."

Sybil looked down at her hands clenched on the wooden railing, then swept her gaze up to the eucalyptus gums overshadowing the wide wooden deck that ran the entire length of the house. I'm over-reacting, she thought. Carol's not still in love with her. It was over long ago.

A fat black and white magpie, tame from regular feeding, looked hopefully down at her, but his greediness didn't raise her usual smile.

How could one phone call put such a cold shadow into the mild sunny spring October day? One call from Christine Tait, and Carol went running to her.

Sybil turned from the railing to pace along the length of the decking. She ignored the spectacular view, knowing if she turned her head she would see in the distance the thrusting tall buildings of central Sydney, if she looked down the steep wooded slope below the house she would be greeted by the wind-ruffled expanse of Middle Harbour as it lay indolent in the warmth of the spring afternoon. She disregarded the scent of wildflowers, the hum of insects busy in the red flare of bottlebrushes and even the lazy plaintive meow from ginger

Jeffrey, who, although comfortably organized in the shade, hated to miss any opportunity for food or attention.

Three years...it had been three years since Christine had told Carol that the affair was over. Wasn't that long enough for Carol to get over her?

She had never met Christine, but had seen numerous photographs of her in the social pages which revealed an attractive, smiling woman with a wide-eyed pleasure in life. This, together with the prominence of her family in politics and business, had made her a favorite in the highest circles of society. Sybil never pointed out these photographs to Carol—not after the first time when she had said, "Isn't this Christine?" and watched Carol's face become austere and turn away from her.

Carol had spoken openly about Christine only once and that had been eight months earlier when Sybil and Carol's relationship was just beginning. Sybil could again feel that stab of jealousy, could shut her eyes and again hear Carol's clear voice telling her with cool economy how Christine had once been the passionate focus of her life: "I loved her so much I was willing to put everything on the line for her..."

An old affair...the sting drawn...the potency gone. But Sybil had watched Carol's expression as she listened to Christine's voice on the telephone. Had watched the way she stood, her hand still on the receiver after the call was over, her face turned away so that all Sybil could see was the swing of her smooth blonde hair. And then Carol's hurried explanation, and not meeting her eyes...

Sybil rubbed the heel of her hand across her forehead. Only now, when their growing relationship was threatened, did she realize quite how much it meant to her. She thought, I'm worrying over nothing. Carol will be back soon and everything will be back to normal...

There was a young woman police officer on crowd control, presenting a self-important human barrier to the people pressed around the entrance to the driveway who were craning their necks in an attempt to see something, anything, of interest.

"I'm sorry, you can't—" she began, stopping in confusion as she recognized Carol in the car. "Oh, Inspector Ashton, I didn't realize..."

The constable hastily waved back the crowd, whose faces were alive with inquisitive stares. Carol heard snatches of words as she edged the car forward through the gates: "It's Carol Ashton...you know, the one who's on television all the time..."

Carol smiled wryly. The Police Commissioner was always keen to have her in the front line of media liaison. As he had put it more than once, "You look good, you sound good and you know what you're talking about—and that's what the Force needs—good PR."

She pulled up behind the untidy row of police vehicles, turned off the ignition and tilted the rear vision mirror to see her own reflection. Would Christine think she had changed? Her green eyes stared back at her, quite calm and objective, a contradiction to the way she felt.

But what did she feel? Anger? Resentment? Apprehension? But not love. Not ever again. She took a deep breath and got out of the car.

The luxurious house was as she remembered it—shaded by substantial trees, set artfully in lush gardens, understated elegance tastefully signaling money and refinement.

Detective Sergeant Mark Bourke stood with a knot of officers on the gravel drive. As he finished his instructions about searching the grounds he saw her. "Carol! What are you doing here? I thought you were off overseas."

"Hello, Mark. Leaving the day after tomorrow."

"Right." He looked at a loss, a frown on his pleasant blunt-featured face.

Of course he must be aware that she had once had a relationship with Christine—must know they had been lovers. He had never mentioned it all the times they had worked together, but she was sure he knew.

She felt a prickly irritation. "Christine Tait's a friend, an old friend. She called me, said Mitchell was dead, and asked me if I'd come."

He half-smiled at her, affectionate. "She's inside with her doctor. Pretty upset. As well she might be, since she and her brother-in-law found her husband's body."

"Any time frame yet?"

Bourke looked pensive. "Last seen about ten-thirty this morning. Found dead round two-thirty this afternoon. Medical's just finished the preliminaries, so we'll have an estimated time of death soon."

Carol said, "Any chance of suicide?"

"Highly unlikely, since there's no sign of the weapon."

The entrance to the house was warm sandstone and cool slate floors. Palms grew from imported Italian earthenware pots. Carol remembered being with Christine the day she chose them and how she had made the man show her pot after pot until she found four perfect ones. Not that he had minded—Chris had smiled charmingly and the man had melted into acquiescence.

The house was full of the familiar bustle of an investigation. People hurried around intent on their appointed tasks: the photographer yawned and packed his gear away; someone made a comment and someone else laughed; the phone rang and was quickly answered by a uniformed officer.

As she walked with Bourke into the front room, he said, "No sign of forced entry. Windows open in here and the back door unlocked." He cleared his throat. "You knew Mitchell Tait." It was a statement, not a question.

Carol nodded. She had known Mitchell well—known his anger, his contempt, and then his triumphant scorn when Christine had decided to stay with him rather than go with Carol.

Ignoring the body on the floor, Carol checked out the room. A grand piano shone satin refinement in one corner; fat pale leather chairs and a matching lounge breathed seemly luxury; the floor gleamed polished richness. Carol could smell the heavy perfume from a huge arrangement of yellow roses crowding a deep blue bowl set exactly in the center of a brass and glass coffee table. Some of the yellow petals had fallen. Chris had always loved roses...

"No sign of a struggle?" she said.

Bourke shook his head. "Not really...a rug over there near the piano is a bit twisted, one of those leather chairs is slightly out of line—that's all." He grinned. "The only really untidy thing around here is Mr. Tait."

In life Mitchell would never have sprawled so casually in front of the imposing black marble fireplace with its elaborate metal firescreen and gleaming brass fire irons, but death had cut the strings that held his dignity intact. As though attempting to hold in the life flowing out of him, he had curled around his wound as he fell and now lay staring down at the blood staining his shirt and trousers, face frozen in agonized astonishment.

"He's been moved for the examination, but that's pretty much how he was found."

They bent over the body, automatically taking care not to touch anything. Bourke said, "Like most stabbings, not a lot of blood. Perhaps a bit more than usual. One wound only, but the weapon was withdrawn, probably straight after the attack, and his heart still had a couple of beats left in it." He pointed

6

out the pattern of blood splatters. "See how a little spurted out between his fingers? He'd already fallen, then. Unfortunately I don't think our murderer is running around soaked in blood."

"Weapon?"

Bourke shook his head. "Nothing yet. Got them searching. Looks like a broad-bladed knife with one cutting edge." He squinted at the wound. "In and twist, I'd say."

Carol looked at Mitchell's contorted face. A hard time dying, she thought. Then: Treat this like any other case. She said, "Suspect?" and waited.

Bourke grinned. "These domestics," he said, shaking his head, "where the husband kills the wife, or the wife kills the husband…"

"You think that applies here?"

Bourke looked as though he had decided, too late, that his levity was out of place. His smile had disappeared as he said, "Carol, you know in situations like this it's odds on to be the wife, or the husband, as the case might be. And there's no sign of forced entry, no report of anyone lurking. Of course, stabbing's risky for a woman, especially if it's not in the back. This guy was a big bloke. Even I'd think twice before taking him on. That means it could be a proxy here—a lover doing the deed on her behalf."

His eyes met Carol's, and he looked momentarily embarrassed. "By lover, I mean…" He cleared his throat and changed the subject. "Tait left his office after ten this morning. Didn't tell his secretary where he was going, or why. Apparently came home here, though nobody's saying they saw him, so we don't know when he arrived, or if he was alone. After two-thirty, Mrs. Tait and Brett Tait, her husband's brother, came in to find him lying dead on the floor. I've got the brother at the local station making a statement, but Mrs. Tait's too upset to speak to me—at least that's what her personal doctor says."

"You doubt she's upset?"

Bourke pursed his lips. "Not at all—but she was self-possessed enough to call her doctor, as well as contacting *you*. And the officers who arrived on the scene first said Mrs. Tait was crying, but okay. It was the brother, Brett, who was in a bad way..." He let his voice trail off and made a face at Carol. "See what you think," he added.

"I'll see Mrs. Tait now," said Carol, finding the formal name strange in her mouth.

Christine was sitting on a blue brocade chair, her head in her hands. Incongruously, she was wearing white tennis clothes and shoes. Carol was vaguely aware that a man was standing beside her, and her mind ticked him off—the doctor—but she didn't look at him. She looked at Christine and Christine dropped her hands and looked up at her.

The moment was almost an anticlimax. It was as though Carol had seen her only yesterday, not three years ago. Her buoyant wavy hair was styled differently, the honey blonde perhaps a little lighter, but the lines of her face, the slate blue eyes, the sensually curved upper lip, the dent in her rounded chin—they were all achingly familiar.

In the past, after the final break, Carol had often wondered what she would say if they ever met again. As it was, her first words were banal. She wouldn't say Christine's name...that would be too personal, and too revealing.

Carol said flatly, "I'm here." She had expected to feel rage, hurt—and perhaps scorn. Anger flared, for a moment, but then she felt calmly fatalistic. Somehow she had always known she would see her again.

Christine had been crying. She looked ravaged, and yet silkenly attractive. The doctor said in a confident medical voice, "Inspector Ashton, I've given Mrs. Tait something to calm her down, so I think questions…" He let his voice trail off.

Carol looked at him for the first time. He was young, smooth, and no doubt successful. She was not surprised that he knew who she was. Even if Christine hadn't mentioned she was coming here, her high profile in the media meant that she was easily recognized. She said, "I'm not here in my official capacity, doctor. I'll only be with Mrs. Tait for a short time."

Christine seemed eager for him to leave, taking his hand and shaking it gently. "You go, Roger—I'm all right."

He was reluctant. "If you say so…Someone will stay with you tonight, will they?"

"Yes. I'll call you tomorrow. You've left me some tablets, so I'll be okay."

After he had gone, there was a silence. Then Christine moved fretfully, saying, "I knew you'd come."

"Did you? I didn't."

"Carol…"

"I haven't any right to expect you to help me. Thank you for being here."

Carol was silent; there was nothing she could say. Christine was nervously pleating the skirt of her tennis dress. "Have you seen him?"

"Mitchell? Yes."

Christine's eyes had filled with tears. "Carol, I can't believe it…that Mitchell's dead…"

Carol felt more secure. This was familiar ground. She said, "I've spoken to Mark Bourke, so I've got some idea of the situation, but it would help if you'd tell me everything from your point of view." She remained standing, forcing Christine to look up at her.

"Oh, Carol, it was horrible…"

"When did you last see Mitchell?"

Christine sat forward in the chair, straightened her shoulders, wiped her eyes. Her voice had the slightest tremor as she replied, "When he left for work this morning. It was just before eight, I think."

"Was there anything unusual? Was he worried? Had he argued with anyone?"

Christine smiled faintly. "You know Mitchell—he has confrontations with people all the time. He made a few phone calls before he left, shouted a bit, demanded action. Just par for the course."

"Conflict with any one person in particular?"

"No."

"Did you have a fight with him?"

The question seemed to astonish Christine. "Did I have a fight with him? Why are you asking me that?"

"When you called me you said, 'They think I killed him.' Why did you say that if you weren't incriminated in some way?"

"I thought…I don't know what I thought. I was shocked. I said the first thing that came into my head…"

Carol resisted the restless impulse to pace. Instead she seated herself opposite Christine. Watching her, she felt relief as she thought, It has gone, that feeling. I can sit here, and look at her, and not feel anything much at all.

She said, "Are you saying there was no conflict between you and Mitchell?"

"No. None."

Deliberately brutal, Carol said, "So where were you when Mitchell was stabbed to death?"

Christine stared at her. "Why are you speaking to me this way?"

"These are the questions Mark Bourke will ask you, but he'll want more detail. He'll want you to account for every moment of the day. Everyone you saw, everyone you spoke to. He'll be particularly interested to find out if you had opportunity to—"

"To what! Kill Mitchell?" She covered her eyes with a hand. "Carol, please…"

It would be so easy to stand, take two steps, put a comforting arm around Christine's shoulders. She leaned back in the chair and said, "What time did you leave the house this morning?"

Christine took a deep breath. "About ten. I drove to Double Bay to do some shopping. After twelve I arrived at a friend's place for lunch. You know her, Carol—Fiona Brandstett. She and John have a place at Darling Point."

"And then?"

"I stayed there till just before two o'clock, then drove here to meet Brett." Her lips began to tremble. "And we found Mitchell…" She shook her head. "I can't talk about it any more."

Carol allowed a measured amount of sympathy into her voice. "Chris, you'll have to talk about it.

"Mitchell was murdered. You could be in danger yourself."

There was a knock at the door. Christine said urgently, "Please help me."

Carol stood, looked down at her, felt the weight of inevitability. She said, "I will, if I can."

Mark Bourke was waiting to speak to Carol. She had left Christine to the care of John and Fiona Brandstett, who had arrived in a cloud of shock and concern.

Bourke said with a grin, "Came in a Roller from the Eastern Suburbs…think we need to know much more about them?"

Carol's tone was dry. "Impressed by the odd Rolls Royce, are you, Mark?"

"Sure am. You know who they are?"

Carol nodded. "Met them, briefly, some years ago."

She had sudden vivid recall of the parties she had attended with Justin, her barrister husband. How he had always checked to see if she had the names pat, the relationships clear, the small talk ready. How she and Christine had traded information, laughed about the gossip and innuendo that flowed in such gatherings. How their friendship had deepened, changed…

Carol said, "Fiona Brandstett's in high society and the one to know if you want to get anywhere in that select little group. Her husband, John, is a partner in Brandstett and Nicholls, a stockbroking firm."

"Good friends to have, under the circumstances," said Bourke cheerfully, "since it makes me so much more reluctant to cause waves by arresting Mrs. Tait for murder."

Carol began to twist the black opal ring she always wore. "You've got something else? Blood? A witness?"

Bourke shook his head. "Not a thing, Carol. It's just a feeling I have. I think she did it."

As Carol turned to go he added, "Medical's given a rough estimate of time of death. Based on room temperature and the cooling of the body, he died about one, give or take half an hour either way."

Carol said, "I think you'll find Mrs. Tait was having lunch with Fiona Brandstett at Darling Point about that time."

"Tsk," said Bourke, "so it *has* to be Mrs. Tait's lover."

Carol drove home, negotiating the thickening late afternoon traffic on the Pacific Highway with her usual smooth efficiency. She felt in control of her emotions and her thoughts. The moment she had dreaded had turned out to be not so bad after all, hadn't it?

Just a few days, to straighten things out, that's all it would take. Surely Sybil would understand why they would have to start their trip overseas a little later than planned. It was true that every day was precious, since Sybil had taken special leave from teaching for their two-month holiday in Europe, but Carol couldn't just leave Christine to face the situation alone, without a friendly voice on the side of the law.

Friendly voice? Somewhere, like a mild toothache, a nagging pain began. "Oh, Chris," she said aloud, then frowned, not knowing why she'd said it.

She walked through the house quietly and came out to the back deck. Sybil hadn't realized she was home, so Carol stood and watched her with affection and something that was almost wistfulness.

Sybil was standing at the railing gazing with bent head down the slope to the sheen of green water far below. The late afternoon sunlight ignited the red of her hair and caught the contour of her cheek.

Carol felt her heart turn. But beauty is always so beguiling, she thought wryly, her eyes running over the lines of Sybil's body. And it isn't enough. It's the person, the person you love...or hate.

Suddenly she felt impatient with herself. What do I want? I know Sybil cares for me—isn't that enough?"

Sybil turned and saw her. "You're back," she said without inflection.

"I'm back," said Carol.

"And?"

Carol shrugged. "And nothing much. Mark Bourke's on the case...I had a look around..."

There was a flash of emotion on Sybil's face. "Don't play games with me, Carol," she said. "Christine...what happened?"

Carol found she didn't want to talk about it, but Sybil's intent gaze made her speak. "Mitchell, her husband, is dead.

He was stabbed while he was home, alone. That's about it, at this stage."

"Carol, you don't have to get involved, do you?"

Sybil's words created a surge of anger in Carol that she knew was illogical; it was directed at herself, at, Sybil, at Christine. "I *am* involved!"

"Why?"

Carol wanted to sound detached. "Mark is playing the percentages—he thinks Christine has something to do with her husband's death because that's the way it works out in so many cases."

"It's what you and Mark Bourke thought in *my* case, when Tony died, isn't it?"

"Yes, initially."

Sybil tried to make her voice less accusatory. "Is there any reason to think Christine did kill him?"

Carol shook her head. "It's too early…but I know she didn't. Chris couldn't do anything like that."

Sybil shrugged. "You didn't give me the benefit of that doubt."

"I didn't know you well, then."

Sybil smiled at her ruefully. "Forgive me. The whole thing must be rather hard for you, and I'm not making it any easier."

"Sybil, when I saw Chris…You don't have to worry…it's all over."

Sybil put her arm around Carol's shoulders and gave her a half hug. "Think it's too early for a drink? After all, we are on holidays."

"Sybil, there's something…"

"What?"

"I just can't abandon Chris—not in the situation she's in. I'm sorry, but I'll have to postpone leaving for a few days."

Sybil forced her voice into polite inquiry. "How many days?"

"Darling, I'm not sure…as soon as I can. Do you want to go on to London and I'll meet you a bit later?"

"No, I'll wait for you. It wouldn't be the same alone."

Carol put a hand up and touched Sybil's cheek. "I'm sorry. Do you understand?"

Sybil thought: Be careful. She said evenly, "Of course."

Chapter 2

The next morning Carol called Mark Bourke very early, before he could leave home. She absent-mindedly counted the number of rings as she stood leaning against the bench that divided the kitchen from the wooden-beamed living room. Through the huge plate glass windows she could see Sybil, crisp in white shorts and T-shirt, coaxing a young kookaburra to take a piece of meat from her fingers. The day was already warm—too warm for October, even if it was spring. "Greenhouse effect," Sybil had said mock-seriously as they had been planning their overseas trip. "Better see the world before the ice caps melt."

Bourke picked up the phone. "Mark? It's Carol. I've a favor to ask."

She knew he would agree—they were good friends, albeit

only within the professional sphere. As she replaced the receiver Sybil came inside.

"While we're away—will the birds leave?"

"Why would they want to? Every time my Aunt Sarah minds the house for me I find them twice as fat when I return."

Sybil's face closed. "Your aunt...have you told her there's a delay?"

"Yes. It's okay with her. She'll come down from her place in the Blue Mountains when we're ready to go."

The words hung on in the air. Carol knew Sybil wanted to say, "How long?" but she didn't speak.

Carol said, "Mark Bourke's coming here later this morning."

"Does he know I've moved in with you?"

Carol shook her head. "I don't know. Don't see how he could, but Mark's surprising—he seems to find things out, almost without meaning to."

"I'll do some shopping this morning anyway, so I won't be here when he comes."

"Sybil, you don't have to..."

"I think it would be easier."

Carol gave her a level look. Sybil knew what she was thinking: Are you ashamed to be with me? To have Mark Bourke know we are lovers?

Sybil silently began to prepare breakfast.

Bourke arrived, brown-suited, neat, his deceptively pleasant self. His easy informality to some extent disguised his abilities at detection. He was keenly observant, painstaking and imaginative—qualities that Carol had valued when they had worked together before.

Carol saw him automatically checking out the rooms as

17

they walked through to the kitchen where the coffee was brewing with loud asthmatic wheezes. She was ridiculously attached to an ancient percolator which she was convinced produced the best coffee ever.

As they sat outside on the wide deck in dappled sunshine, mugs of coffee at hand, Carol made a decision. "Mark, I think you should know Sybil Quade is living with me."

"I know, Carol." He grinned at her raised eyebrows. "At the trial I thought...Well, I'm a detective, remember?" His smile faded as he added, "And perhaps it'll make it easier if I tell you I also know about your relationship with Christine Tait."

"That was over long ago. I haven't seen her for three years. Then she rang me...I feel I should help her—"

"For old times' sake?"

Carol nodded. "Yes. For old times' sake. That's all, Mark."

Mark Bourke leaned back in the deep wooden deck chair in an unsuccessful attempt to look at ease. "Carol, it makes things difficult..." He made a face at her. "If you get involved in this case...there's a clear conflict of interest..."

"I'm just asking you to keep me informed of everything. I'm on leave. It'd be unofficial."

"You can't possibly be objective about this one."

Carol was infuriated by his tone, but her voice remained neutral. "You're being paid to be objective, Mark—I'm just Christine's friend. Okay?"

He relaxed and smiled. "Okay."

Carol took notes as he succinctly recounted the information he had gathered so far. On Wednesday morning Mitchell Tait had driven to his company's offices in North Sydney. Between nine and ten he had been in a meeting with his two partners. He had left the offices about ten-thirty, telling his secretary he would be back later in the afternoon. He had mentioned no names and gave no indication of where he might be going.

As yet Bourke hadn't yet found anyone who saw Tait from that point onwards. The drive was about twenty minutes to half an hour to his home in Lindfield, so if he had gone straight there he would have arrived about eleven o'clock.

"It's not the type of neighborhood," said Bourke, "where you chat over the fence or drop in to borrow a cup of sugar. Door-knocking the street's been pretty fruitless—I get the impression polite indifference to one's neighbors is regarded as the only way to behave." He grinned, adding, "The immediate neighbors of the Taits seemed almost as shocked by the idea that they might pry as they were by the fact of Tait's murder. In short, nobody admits to seeing anything. The time of death was approximately one o'clock, so if he had gone directly home, Mitchell Tait would have had about two hours to fill in before he was stabbed. He had taken off his suit coat and was in his shirtsleeves when attacked. The stabbing seemed to be a surprise, as cuts on his hands appeared to be inflicted as the knife was withdrawn when he was dying, not in any attempt at self-defense."

"Still no weapon?" said Carol.

Bourke shook his head. "Not yet. Seems to have been a broad-bladed knife, quite substantial. Did a lot of damage with one thrust and a twist or two. Not a heat of the moment gosh-I-hate-you, but more a premeditated execution."

"Ever colorful in your descriptions," said Carol with a half-smile, which faded as Bourke gave more details of the preliminary medical report. No one could have saved Mitchell Tait once he was stabbed. The knife had inflicted devastating injuries to his liver, lungs and chest cavity, so that it was a race as to whether he drowned in his own blood or died as his blood pressure dropped from massive internal bleeding.

Again they discussed the probability of blood splattering onto the murderer, but as it was a single blow with the weapon and not a series of slashes or stab wounds, there was comparatively little external blood.

"The only traces of human blood in the place, apart from on the corpse, were in the drain pipe of the kitchen sink," said Bourke, "so our murderer probably washed knife and hands before disappearing off into the blue." He stretched and grinned. "And regrettably no reports of maniacs brandishing large knives whilst running around the neighborhood, in case you were going to ask."

"Do you still have Christine Tait as your main suspect?"

Bourke's expression became stubborn. "Look, Carol, I haven't any pre-conceived ideas of her guilt, or her innocence. I hope to be interviewing her later today. I think you should know, however, that there are rumors of trouble in the marriage."

"What sort of trouble?"

"The name that keeps coming up is Brett Tait, her brother-in-law...and, incidentally, the person by her side when she discovered her husband's body."

"Meaning?"

"Carol, you're not her defense lawyer. You know very well how often an inconvenient spouse is disposed of with the help of a lover."

She was nettled by his tone. She raised her eyebrows, saying, "So there are absolutely no other suspects?"

His good humor restored by Carol's sarcasm, Bourke made an expansive gesture. "Suspects? Practically coming out of the woodwork." He beamed at Carol's impatient expression. "Mitchell Tait," he said, "was the perfect murderee. If his wife didn't get him, several of his business associates would have queued up for the pleasure. And it's a measure of how much dislike he generated in certain people that I got all this information in a few hours late yesterday afternoon. Obviously he could be an absolute bastard. Mind you, not everyone held this negative view—his secretary was in tears, and one of his partners, Gloria Tyne, was too upset to speak to me."

Carol didn't comment. She knew Bourke would follow up every person, every lead, every hint of love or hate. She thought back to the Mitchell Tait she had known. He had been a large man in every way, ambitious and driving. She remembered his impatient staccato voice, his thick black springy hair, the way he tapped his fingers with irritation at any delay, the field of sheer energy that vibrated around him, the threatening atmosphere he could create if anyone or anything stood in his way.

"People as successful as he was in business often make enemies."

Bourke shrugged agreement. "Sure they do, but it seems Mitchell Tait wasn't only ruthless to competitors, he was prepared to ride roughshod over his partners, too."

Mitchell Tait, with two others, had started TTB Computing, initially a small company specializing in communications software. Well-managed, aggressive in the marketplace and peddling inspired products, it had grown at a phenomenal rate and Tait had decided, against the other partners' wishes, to go public and try for a listing on the Stock Exchange.

"I'll be seeing the two partners later this morning, so I'll have more details then."

"You'll give me what you get?"

Bourke smiled at her. "Carol, you'll get everything I get… more, you'll get my invaluable analysis of it all!"

Carol looked up from her notes as Sybil came into the room, saying as she put a bag of groceries on the bench, "Safe for me to come in?"

With the slightest edge to her voice, Carol said, "Mark's gone, if that's what you mean."

Sybil sat beside her and put an arm around her waist. "I'm sorry. You know I'll do anything to avoid even the hint of a confrontation."

As Carol lightly kissed her cheek, the phone rang. Sybil picked up the receiver. Her face blank, she handed it to Carol. "It's for you."

"Who was that?" said Christine's voice.

Carol ignored the question. "What's wrong?"

"I want to see you, Carol. Please."

"Has something else happened?"

There was a hint of hysteria in Christine's tone. "I know someone's trying to frame me for Mitchell's murder. Is that enough for you?"

"Where are you?"

She replaced the receiver and looked up into Sybil's guarded eyes. "Christine says someone is trying to frame her."

"Who? Why?"

Carol shook her head. "Don't know. I'm going to see her to find out. Here's the address and telephone number if you need me. Belongs to the Brandstetts where she's staying at the moment."

Sybil watched her as she went to change, angry that all Christine had to do was demand, and Carol obeyed.

After Carol had gone Sybil threw some things into a sports bag, placated both Jeffrey and Carol's slimmer cat Sinker with a snack each (strategically distanced) and drove to the self-satisfied streets of the neighboring suburb of Mosman.

Everywhere jacaranda trees had burst into their purple mists of flowers and the wind had blown fallen petals into purple shadows under their flaunting branches. There was that indefinable lift in the air that spoke of spring and promise and summer nights to come.

Mosman was a favored area, close to the city, full of mansions restored to their former glories, tasteful boutiques, and the scent of money. It also possessed a beautiful harbor beach, Balmoral, proximity to which was highly prized.

As it was Thursday, most people were at work, but well-groomed Mosman matrons, with and without designer-clad offspring, had angle-parked their sleek cars and arranged themselves to partake of the sun and sand, and, just possibly, the water.

Marking her personal space on the sand with towel and bag, Sybil stripped to her black bikini and walked down to the water's edge.

Black for mourning, she thought. She gave herself a mental shake. Because she loved Carol, and because she was alarmed at Christine's reappearance on the. scene, she had allowed herself to behave like a possessive child. A relationship had to be built on trust—and she trusted Carol.

She began to saunter along the shoreline, watching her feet as the water sucked and swirled. Although Balmoral Beach lay deep within Sydney Harbour, it often had a miniature surf because it was situated directly opposite the two massive headlands that marked the entrance, and in a heavy sea the Pacific swell rolled in causal blue-green waves to break on its white sands.

When she was depressed or upset she always went to the water and the sand to be soothed by the restless constancy of the ocean. Today the medicine wasn't working. As she thought of Carol meeting Christine, talking to her, perhaps touching her hand, she felt a stab of helpless jealousy.

She waded out into the green of the water, forcing herself to concentrate on the shock of the coldness against her warm body. She swam with rapid strokes, efficient and strong against the lazy power of the water, then, chilled, came out to lie in the warm sun.

Eyes closed, her thoughts centered on Christine. What if she *had* killed her husband…would Carol still stand by her? Sybil found herself actively hoping Christine was guilty and that any moment now she would break down and confess.

Then she was ashamed of herself. She knew from first-hand experience the dark terror of murder and the threat of violence. Why glibly wish that the whole thing be disposed of like the neat ending of an Agatha Christie mystery? Life wasn't like that, tidy and satisfying; it was messy and confusing and people loved and hated in ways that you couldn't control.

She thought of last night and bit her lip. They had been so careful with each other, so cautious not to disturb the peace. When they had gone to bed, Carol had kissed her, said she was tired and turned her back to go to sleep. Sybil wanted to curl around her, to cuddle her and say, "I feel threatened because you're seeing Christine again." Instead she listened to Carol's even breathing, knowing she was awake too and unwilling to acknowledge it. Eventually she drifted into an uneasy sleep, dreaming uncomfortable visions that faded in the morning light but left a hangover of uncertainty and sadness.

Sybil thought, How should I behave? What should I say and do? Then she was impatient with herself—why did she always try to protect herself by working out ways people might react and what might happen? She should know by now there was no way to be sure what anything would lead to—no way to predict what someone might say or do or feel. Strangely, she had a sudden vivid picture of Tony and the sterility of their marriage. What real emotion, what true communication, had there ever been in that?

And yet Carol…she cared more for Carol than she had ever cared for anyone, perhaps ever would care. It wasn't Carol's smooth blonde hair and her green eyes and the classic planes of her face, it wasn't her eager passion, or even her keen

24

intelligence—it was *her*, the real Carol, the person underneath the skin. That was the Carol she loved.

Loved, yes—but how willing had she been to commit herself to the relationship? The intense desire for self-protection, her ingrained reluctance to let go and be vulnerable, had made her unwilling, almost unable, to enter into a full and open-hearted relationship with Carol.

Although lovers almost from the beginning, it had only been four weeks ago that Sybil had taken the step of renting out her own house and moving in with Carol. They had developed a pleasant, easy-going routine and an often passionate, but somehow not intensely personal, way of relating. Comfortable, non-threatening—but now that urge to protect herself, to keep something in reserve, had boomeranged.

Christine's appeal for help had made Sybil keenly aware that she felt more for Carol than she had realized...but it had also made it impossible for her to tell this to Carol. Under threat, her own instincts were always to withdraw. What made it so hard to do this now were the unsuspected depths of emotion she was finding in herself.

A depression, metallic and hard, settled about her, its darkness reflecting into the bright day.

It seemed incredible that she had only known Carol for nine months. "I can't bear it if this is all I'll have," Sybil said aloud, but only a seagull heard her words.

The harborside Eastern Suburbs area of Sydney looked upon the North Shore with scornful superiority, secure in the arrogance that old money and strong connections could give. Carol raised an eyebrow at the very social St. Mark's Church as she passed it: she had been married there. She remembered Justin's pleasure at the wedding—the weather perfect, the guest list impeccable, the bride and groom ready to stride into a golden future.

Later, Justin's second marriage had been small and private, officiated over by a polished marriage celebrant—Justin's correction to his regrettable error in marrying a latent lesbian.

She had a sudden disturbing thought: If Christine was charged with Mitchell's murder, would she turn to Justin Hart for help? But surely Justin would refuse...Yet, he knew the value of publicity. It was not by accident that he was widely known as one of the most brilliant defense lawyers in Sydney, if not in all Australia.

Carol shook her head. It wouldn't—it couldn't—come to that. Chris wouldn't be charged; the real murderer would be found. Mark Bourke was good, very good. His success rate was excellent and there was no reason to suppose he was going to fail with this case.

The streets of Darling Point were lined with European trees that irritated the inhabitants with the unnecessary shedding of their leaves in Sydney's mild winter. Even so, the trees were not replaced with natives—this was an area where the traditions of civilization included the vegetation of cultures half a world away. Many of the houses and blocks of flats were unprepossessing and old-fashioned, but somehow it didn't matter; well-tended gardens burst with flowers, and the glimpses of the harbor, shimmering blue in the glaring light, reminded the observer of the favored location—close to Sydney city, to exclusive yacht clubs, to the cosmopolitan elegance (and expense) of the Double Bay shopping area.

The Brandstetts owned the top floor of an extremely ugly but very well-positioned block of luxury units. Obviously built some time ago and designed by an architect with a taste for ostentatious stonework, the five apartments, one on top of the other, gazed with window walls across Double Bay to the even more exclusive suburb of Point Piper. Because of the steep slope of the land at the edge of the small headland that formed Darling Point, the top two units rose above the road level; the other three nestled into the slope below.

The metallic blue BMW parked in the visitors' area had a personalized number plate: CHRIS. The name tightened Carol's stomach muscles. She wanted to be reluctant to be here, and yet there was an undercurrent of excitement in the prospect of seeing Christine again.

She punched the button marked Brandstett with unnecessary force. There was a delay, a splutter of voice, and then, almost before Carol could respond, the buzzer sounded to indicate the security doors had been unlocked.

Faced with the shiny coffin of a narrow elevator for the one floor journey, Carol chose the stairs. The heavy polished door was opened by a woman obviously in the process of house cleaning. Her acquaintance with English seemed scant, and she interrupted Carol's polite words with an emphatic gesture directed at the floor: "Down there...pool...down there."

Carol rode down in the elevator, faintly alarmed at its rheumatic creakings as it made its way slowly down to the bottom floor. She stepped out to an expanse of artificial grass, a selection of real palm trees and a large rectangular aquamarine swimming pool surrounded by white furniture. Over a low stone wall yachts swung at their moorings and across the little bay a helicopter fussed over landing on a floating helipad. There were only two people in the pool area. Mrs. Brandstett reclined on a lounge; Christine swam docilely in the pool.

As Carol approached, Fiona Brandstett rose, advancing with a small smile. "Inspector," she said formally, "I hope you had no trouble finding us. I gave strict instructions to Imelda, but, of course...English..." Her slight shrug implied resigned wonder that one should neglect to fully master the language of one's employers.

27

From the pool Chris waved acknowledgment. Fiona Brandstett put a restraining hand on Carol's arm. "Before you speak to Christine, I'd like a word with you."

It had been years since they had last met and clearly Fiona Brandstett was not going to refer to their slight acquaintance of the past. Carol appraised her. Fiona Brandstett was as slim as low impact aerobics and chrome exercise machines could make her. Her pallid hair was beautifully styled and her fingernails perfectly painted in a delicate rose. Dressed in coordinated cream linen slacks and top, she exuded an air of patrician elegance. Carol estimated she was in her mid-forties, though it was hard to be sure, since obviously she had on her side the resources of money, time and determination.

She was saying: "…sure you will appreciate what a dreadful shock it has been for Christine…"

On cue, Carol nodded. Fiona continued, "And I've told her we both want her to stay here with us indefinitely, but she insists on going back home…" Her expression indicated the folly of such an action.

Another pause for Carol to acknowledge her words. Mulishly, Carol refused to do so, merely waiting for Fiona to continue.

"Inspector, I wonder if you would bring your influence, both as a friend and as a police officer, to persuade her to stay here with us."

Carol's expression didn't change, but she was aware of the slight emphasis on "friend" was intended to have a sting. "Surely," she said pleasantly, "that's up to her."

Fiona Brandstett permitted a feather of irritation to brush her face. "You think she's safe? In that house where Mitchell was brutally murdered?"

"I don't imagine she'd stay there alone."

"But that is precisely what she intends to do. You agree it could be dangerous?"

Carol was puzzled by the motivation behind the conversation. There seemed to be something other than just concern for Christine's safety. Fiona must have suspected some hint of this was on her face, for she said abruptly, "No matter. Christine must make her own mind up, of course."

Carol said, as they walked towards the pool, "You knew Mitchell Tait well?"

"Of course. My husband and I would count ourselves as close friends of the Taits. Also, John and Mitchell had business connections. It's a great tragedy."

Her voice gave no clue as to her opinion of the depth of the tragedy. She stopped and said, "Christine is, of course, devastated. Frankly, we are all devastated."

Carol made a mental note to check on any business dealings John Brandstett had had with Mitchell Tait. There might be a motive here.

Christine swam to the edge of the pool and swung herself onto the tiles with one graceful movement. Her rose pink bikini was brief, her skin lightly tanned, her body as lithe as Carol remembered it. Unwelcome, a memory insinuated itself: caressing Chris in the heat of passion, sliding her hands over her shoulders, down her back...

"Has Fiona told you?" asked Chris.

"Sorry?"

"Told you I was definitely here, yesterday..."

Fiona said firmly, "Every Wednesday Christine and I play tennis with a small group of friends. Christine usually comes here and we have a light lunch first. Yesterday was no exception." She paused to review Carol's reaction. "I have already told the police the details."

Carol nodded. Fiona continued, "Christine arrived early, actually. I was still doing my laps of the pool. I do them most days before lunch."

"What time was this?"

Fiona gave the question consideration, as though it was a new thought. "Time? A few minutes after noon."

"How do you know that?"

"I beg your pardon?"

Carol was sweetly patient. "How did you know the time if you were doing laps of the pool?"

A satisfied smile from Fiona. "Detective Sergeant Bourke asked the same thing. I time my laps closely—I wear a waterproof watch/stopwatch."

Christine had observed the exchange with the faintest trace of a smile. "Don't you believe I tell the truth?"

Carol's tone was even. "It's not believing, it's proving that's important. What time did you go to play tennis?"

Christine looked to Fiona, who said, "Chris was tired and I had a slight headache. We decided to indulge ourselves and have a lazy afternoon."

"You spent most of the time down here at the swimming pool?"

"No. We had a light lunch and stayed upstairs, chatting."

Carol said, "Any visitors or telephone calls?" Fiona gave her a tight smile. "No."

Christine moved listlessly. "I left here just before two o'clock. That's what you're working up to, isn't it?"

Carol looked into Christine's slate-blue eyes. "If the times are accurate, then you must know you have a strong alibi. No one could possibly frame you. What made you think someone would?"

Twisting her hands together, Christine said urgently, "Please, Carol…this is a nightmare. The questions Detective Bourke asked Brett…it seems as if he's trying to make out that we…that we did it together."

Carol said to Fiona, "Are you absolutely certain about the times?"

"I'm not in the habit of lying," said Fiona with frozen

disapproval.

An irrational dislike rising in her, Carol thought, Like hell you aren't! Isn't polite society just a series of lies?

Christine's fingers brushed Carol's hand. "Can you tell me? Do the police know exactly when Mitchell died?"

Carol's skin burned where she had been touched. She said, "Unfortunately it isn't possible to be absolutely accurate—it's more an informed guess."

"I was here with Fiona when he died, Carol."

Carol nodded. "How long does it take to drive from here to Lindfield? Half an hour? Forty minutes?"

"It depends on the traffic, but always more than half an hour. On Wednesday, though, as I mentioned to you, I didn't drive straight from home. I left early and did some shopping at Double Bay."

"When Mitchell arrived you had already gone?"

"I've already told you I didn't see him!"

Fiona interrupted. "Shall we go inside for refreshments?"

As Fiona collected her things, Carol said to Christine, "You said on the phone someone was trying to frame you. Who would want to? Is there something you haven't told me?"

Christine lowered her voice. "I don't want to discuss it here."

"Then why did you ask me to come over?"

Christine looked away. "I wanted…I needed to see you. I'm frightened, Carol. I don't know what's happening. You're not involved. You're the only person I feel I can trust."

"Shall we go?" said Fiona, joining them.

The metal box of the elevator had room for them all, but Fiona insisted on climbing the stairs. Chris said, as the elevator began its geriatric climb, "Fiona never misses an opportunity to keep fit. She always uses the stairs. It's part of her daily routine. So many laps of the pool, a run up the stairs, a session at the gym—all far too exhausting for me."

There was silence for a moment, then Christine said, "Who answered the phone when I rang this morning?"

Carol was casual. "A friend."

"Anyone I know?"

"No."

Carol was conscious of Chris's every breath, the brush of her arm, the scent of her body in the enclosed space. She wanted the elevator to hurry, but it continued upward at a maddeningly slow pace. "Are there only five floors? This is taking forever."

Christine looked at her enigmatically. "Can't wait to get away from me, eh?"

The door split open at the top floor just as Fiona arrived, a little out of breath, at the top of the stairs, so Carol was able to avoid any answer.

The Brandstett's unit was large, illuminated by the sunlight striking through the plate glass, and furnished in a style that was all angles, glass and metal. Carol noted the couple of Brett Whiteleys and a Dobell on the walls. Through the wide windows she could see the helicopter across the bay humming like an angry metallic mosquito as it prepared to launch itself into the air. Imelda and her broken English had vanished, leaving the expansive surfaces of metal and glass antiseptically gleaming. Everything had a place, and was in it.

Fiona was rapidly on hand with a selection of imported biscuits, bread sticks, pate, smoked salmon and other delicacies. Tea, coffee or something harder was offered. Christine, who was looking progressively more strained, asked for a gin and tonic; Fiona had a cup of Earl Gray tea, Carol had coffee, both brews served in bone china cups of undoubted expense but repellent pattern.

"This evening," said Christine, her voice husky with fatigue, "I'm going home. I telephoned Detective Bourke this morning and he says the police have finished there. Besides, I can't impose on Fiona and John any more." She waved away Fiona's protest. "No, really, Fee, you've been wonderful, but I've had all the door and window locks changed this morning, and I'm sure I'll be perfectly safe."

The front door slammed. Carol watched Christine jump at the sound and Fiona slowly turn her head.

"Fee? Where the bloody hell are you? It's me!"

A bustle, the sound of a briefcase hitting the floor, and John Brandstett strode into the room. Seeing Carol, he stopped, a puzzled frown on his face.

His wife gracefully snatched the conversational ball. "Inspector, of course you know my husband. Darling, you remember Inspector Carol Ashton..."

"Carol, is it? Right!"

He pumped her hand twice, then released it abruptly. He had sticky hands. She thought he'd been drinking. His face was flushed and his nose was beginning to take on the purplish color of a heavy imbiber. He had slightly bulging pale blue eyes and a loud, hectoring voice. His clothing, however, was in strong contrast to the coarseness of his manner—a beautifully cut dark gray suit and silk shirt and a muted tie indicating membership in an exclusive city club.

Carol amused herself briefly by considering how he should be dressed to match his manner. She clothed him in a grubby T-shirt bearing an obscenely sexist message and a pair of crumpled shorts.

He seemed unable to speak in a normal volume, bellowing at his wife, "Aren't you ready? I'm here to take you both to lunch. Put off important appointments to do this, so get a move on."

If Fiona found this embarrassing, not a hint crossed her face. She said, "Christine insists she's going home this evening."

Her husband had gone straight to the bar and was pouring himself a large whiskey. "Drinks, anyone?" Fiona's words sank in and he turned in red-faced consternation. "What? Won't hear of it, Chris! Not safe. Madman loose." He swung his prominent eyes to Carol. "Don't you agree? You being the police?"

Christine said, "It's all right, John. Carol's going to check out the house before I move back."

Carol maintained a detached expression as Chris gave her a tentative smile.

Fiona Brandstett said, "Chris, no! You must stay here."

"Fee, please. I want to go."

Fiona's patrician shrug managed to encompass opposition, irritation and reluctant compliance.

Christine said to Carol, "Could you meet me at the house at seven? Would that be possible? Please?"

"I hoped to be seeing David tonight."

Carol had arranged sometime previously to see her nine-year-old son this Thursday evening, instead of the usual weekend, because on Friday she and Sybil had intended to fly out to London.

Frowning, Christine said, "But you always used to see him on the weekends."

"This was special. I was going away tomorrow." Alarm flared in Christine's face. "Away? Are you? Where?"

"It doesn't matter, I've put it back a few days."

"Well, since you're not going, couldn't you see David some other time? Carol, it means a lot to me."

Why not? thought Carol. I have to talk to her alone, and the sooner, the better.

She nodded agreement, made arrangements to meet at seven and thanked the Brandstetts for their hospitality. Fiona accomplished a polite but markedly cool farewell, John Brandstett bustled her to the door, showering almost incoherent comments.

He's drinking, Carol thought, drinking a lot. I wonder why.

Chapter 3

Sybil's car was absent from the street level carport, but someone had parked in her place. Carol drew in smoothly beside the station wagon as a dark-suited man got out of the driver's seat to greet her.

"Carol?"

"Hello, Brett."

"It's so long since I've seen you...Hope you don't mind... Chris said you were helping her..."

"Are you coming in?"

Brett Tait followed her down the steep flower-edged path, still explaining. "Chris said I should talk to you. Carol, I can't believe it...what's happened to Mitchell...and the police, they suspect..."

It had been three years since Carol had seen Brett, and

his brother's death had obviously affected him deeply. Even so, although his face was gaunt and strained, his height had never given him authority—it merely reinforced the gangly little-boy look that Carol remembered so well. The same lock of straight brown hair fell across his forehead, and he used the same nervous scoop of his fingers to push it back into place. She found herself watching the repeated gesture with irritation as she settled him into a chair.

Brett resembled his brother facially—he had the same heavy brows, deep-set eyes and angular jaw—but otherwise he was younger, thinner, more handsome and less successful. Brett had resisted Mitchell's suggestions that he join TTB Computing, instead setting up a business of his own specializing in the import of curtain and upholstery fabrics. Although Mitchell had injected substantial capital into Brett's business, the cut-throat world of home furnishings had been a difficult field in which to court success and three years ago Brett had been struggling to establish himself in the market.

"How's your business going?" she asked.

He didn't seem surprised at the question, saying readily, "Not too good, actually. Keeping my head above water, but it hasn't turned out to be the money-spinner I hoped."

He started to explain the trials and tribulations of a small business owner, not with any great conviction, but as though it was a way of avoiding the real issue he had come to discuss. Carol half-listened, her thoughts on Mark Bourke's flippant words that morning: "Often an inconvenient spouse is disposed of with the help of a lover."

Brett and Chris together? Although she had to admit it wasn't impossible, Carol thought it was the kind of risk Christine would never run. After all, she had refused, when it came to the crunch, to leave Mitchell for Carol…Would she even think of leaving her dynamic husband for his decidedly unsuccessful younger brother?

Yet Brett *was* attractive, in his little-boy way. The contrast of his dark suit and subdued tie with his air of vulnerability was oddly engaging. Her attention was caught as he said Christine's name.

"…but it's Chris who's important, not me." He pushed the lock of hair back. "Detective Bourke's questioned me twice, and he thinks, I know he thinks, that Chris and I…" A helpless gesture finished the sentence.

"Are lovers?"

"Carol, it isn't true! I'm fond of her, of course—we've always got on well—but that's all. And to say I'd have anything to do with Mitchell's death…"

"Where were you yesterday afternoon?"

Brett spread his hands. "Carol! That's the trouble. I don't know if I can prove where I was. I saw prospects in the morning out Parramatta way. About lunchtime, just after twelve, I stopped for a hamburger at a McDonald's. I was there about three quarters of an hour, I suppose. Struck up a conversation with a woman who was a rep selling pool chemicals, but although I've given the police all the details, I didn't get her name, or what company she works for, so I suppose it's pretty hopeless."

Brett's good looks had meant that he always managed to have an attractive female in tow, although he never seemed able to settle into a long-term relationship. Carol thought that the woman, if she existed, might well remember the conversation.

"And the rest of the time?" she asked.

Brett slumped his shoulders in defeat. "It's just about impossible to substantiate where I was. I only have one other person in the office, to answer the phone. Yesterday morning I went there first, did some paperwork, and set out a bit after nine to call on prospects. For a lot of the time I was just driving."

"Did you actually have firm appointments?"

He was eager to please. "In the morning, yes. And they'll say I was there, but there's a lot of time I can't account for."

"When, exactly?"

He looked miserable and defiant at the same time. "If they don't find that pool chemicals girl, I don't think I can prove where I was between twelve and two-fifteen...After that I was with Chris. Frankly, during the day I got a bit depressed. I wasn't getting any joy at any of the prospects I visited, so I'd driven a long way for nothing. I seemed to be banging my head against a brick wall, so I just drove around, did a bit of shopping, that sort of thing."

"And went to McDonald's. Which one?"

"Church Street, Parramatta. A long way from Mitchell's place. And I wouldn't even have known he was home." He made another gesture of helplessness.

Carol kept the irritation out of her voice. "Apart from your conversation with the woman, did anything unusual happen? Did you argue about the change? Have any sort of disagreement? Anything like that?"

Brett shook his head. "No. The cops asked me the same thing. Carol, nobody is going to remember me—but I was there, really I was—when Mitchell was killed."

Carol was interested to know why he was with Christine during the afternoon. Brett explained that she had asked him to meet her at the house at two-fifteen, saying that she'd be playing tennis earlier.

"So Christine made the suggestion you meet together?"

"Yes, but I'd already said it was terribly important to see her."

"Why?"

Brett licked his lips. "Look, Carol, this is why we need you. It was about money."

Carol's silence drew the reluctant words from him. "The

fact is," he said, "I am in a bit of trouble with the business. Need capital fast, or I'll go under. I asked Mitchell for help, but he said he'd sunk enough cash into it." He essayed a rueful smile. "Said I should sink or swim, and he rather thought I'd sink."

"Why was Christine involved?"

"Chris? She was a darling about it all. She couldn't see why Mitchell wouldn't help me. It wasn't as if he wasn't rolling in it…" He paused to consider his tone, modifying it to remove the resentment as he continued, "She thought we should get together and plan an approach…you know, Chris would soften Mitchell up a bit…I'd show him how I could trade out of the temporary difficulties…that sort of thing."

Carol let the silence last for a moment, then said, "Do you inherit from Mitchell?"

Frowning, Brett pressed his lips together. "Why?" he said with a trace of belligerence.

"Because it gives you a motive. The investigation will cover everything, Brett, including your brother's will."

Brett threw up his hands. "Christ!"

Carol waited. He met her eyes with a grimace. "If Mitchell didn't change his will, yes, I do get something."

"Much?"

He smiled grimly. "Enough to give me a motive? I suppose so."

Carol let her impatience show. "Look, Brett, you've got quite enough brains to work all this out for yourself. Now, what's the real reason you came to see me?"

Brett settled back in his chair. His face grew harder. "You've got influence, Carol. God, you're a Detective Inspector, yet! You're on the inside and I can see things look a bit dicey for Chris and me. I want to know if you're willing to help us."

"Chris has an alibi."

Brett leaned forward. "Perhaps she has," he said, "but that

wouldn't make her any less guilty if we planned it together and I carried it out."

"Which you didn't."

He sighed. "I know it looks bad, but I loved Mitchell, and so did Chris. We didn't plan to kill him. We didn't kill him. We had nothing to do with it, but it's the most obvious way for the cops to think…That's why we need you."

Carol wondered if his concern was for himself alone, but that he had included Christine in order to insure Carol's assistance. She said soothingly, "It's very early in the investigation and Detective Bourke's job is to chase down every possible lead or suspicion. That's all he's doing. I wouldn't worry too much."

She saw him out, adroitly avoiding committing herself to any special pleading on his behalf. She thought, Tonight I'll ask Chris about Brett…all about Brett.

Carol rang Eleanor, her ex-husband's second (and more satisfactory) wife, to arrange to pick David up on Sunday morning, rather than that night. Then she sat staring at the list of questions she wanted Chris to answer. One question was not written down, one she couldn't even frame in words.

I congratulated myself too early, she reflected, I saw Christine and I didn't feel anything much…But now…what am I feeling now?

She heard Sybil's car and found she was bracing herself for the meeting. She rose, self-contained, to greet her, but underneath she was sharply aware of confusion and disharmony.

Sybil kissed her, being careful, Carol thought, not to vary the routine.

Carol said, "I have to go out tonight. I've put David off until Sunday morning."

Sybil didn't ask where she was going, but the question ached to be answered. Carol found herself saying, "I'm seeing Christine."

"Again?"

She had to smile at the protesting tone. "Yes, it does seem a bit much, doesn't it? She inveigled me into it, actually, in front of the Brandstetts."

Sybil's arching eyebrows expressed surprise. Carol was fleetingly amused at Sybil's skill in extracting information from her. After all, wasn't *she* the professional interrogator?

Carol said, "I need to see her alone, where she can be frank, where she can tell me the truth."

Sybil waited.

Carol wanted to explain. "Apparently there are rumors that Christine and Brett Tait, Mitchell's brother, are lovers. Brett was here a few minutes ago, asking me to put in a good word for them. Brett doesn't have an alibi and he's worried. It looks like it was impossible for Christine to have murdered Mitchell, but even so I just want to make sure he doesn't try to drag her into it in an effort to save his neck."

"What gives Christine a safe alibi?"

"Mitchell almost certainly died somewhere between twelve-thirty and one-thirty—for convenience, let's say one o'clock. Christine arrived at Fiona Brandstett's in Darling Point just after twelve and stayed there for almost two hours, so there's no way she could be killing him and there at the same time."

Sybil slid onto one of the stools at the breakfast bar. "How can you be sure he died then?" She indicated the morning paper spread open on the bench. *Society Husband Stabbed* announced the headline, continuing in smaller print *Mystery of the Missing Hours*. "The paper says nobody saw him or spoke to him from the time he left his office in the morning."

"Do you really want to know the details?"

Sybil said, "I remember when Tony died you could only narrow it down to a couple of hours. Why is it possible to be more accurate this time?"

"Because Mitchell was killed inside, where the temperature remained reasonably constant. A dead body cools at a fixed rate, and although this can be influenced by the surrounding conditions and temperature, in Mitchell's case it gave a fairly accurate estimate of the time of death. There are other factors, of course. For example, digestion stops abruptly upon death, so calculations can be made from the last meal the person ate. Rigor mortis is another—but Mitchell's body was discovered before the stiffening began, and anyway, it can vary widely."

Carol was amused at Sybil's expression. "A little more detail than you required, perhaps?" she queried.

"It's not that. It reminds me…"

Carol felt contrite. "Darling, I'm sorry, but you did ask."

Sybil made a face at her. "I did." She swung off the barstool and put an arm around Carol. "If Christine has an alibi for the time her husband was murdered, do you really need to stay?"

"Yes, I do."

"Don't you trust Mark Bourke to conduct a fair investigation?"

Carol was prickly and defensive. "Of course. But she asked me for help."

"Help? Does she really need it?"

Anger flared in Carol. "Don't push it!"

Sybil let her arm drop and stepped back. There was a silence as both of them considered the shifting ground. Finally Sybil said tentatively, "Carol?"

"Yes?"

Sybil looked half apologetic, half resigned as she finally said, "I don't know the rules for this situation, Carol. I don't know what to say or do."

Carol felt suddenly weary. "Neither do I."

It was a relief to have the interruption of the telephone. Carol picked up the receiver to hear Mark Bourke's cheerful voice.

"Got a pen?" he said, "I'm a positive fount of information. Firstly, Mitchell Tait's will is rather interesting…"

Christine was to inherit the house, a holiday home at Pearl Beach and half of the other assets. Brett Tait gained two hundred thousand dollars. There were various bequests to charities and distant relatives.

"And a positively fascinating touch," said Bourke, "has to do with the control of TTB Computing. Mitchell Tait has given one of the two remaining partners a controlling interest."

"Let me guess," said Carol. "The female partner?"

Bourke laughed. "Indeed so! Gloria Tyne by name. She was too upset to see me yesterday, but I saw her this morning—not that I gained much from the interview. Now that I know Tait thought she was worth giving control of his company to, I have the liveliest interest in seeing her again."

Bourke gave Carol brief details of Tait's two partners. Gloria Tyne was widely regarded in the industry as a technical genius who had materially contributed to the success of TTB Computing with the innovative communications software programs she created. She shared equal partnership with Kurt Boardman, who handled the sales side of the business. However, since Mitchell Tait was the senior and founding partner, he had more say in the company's direction. An entrepreneur, he had driven the business to greater and greater success, not only by his management, but by the financial resources he attracted.

"Any motives strong enough to kill?" asked Carol.

"Could be. As I mentioned this morning, there was a lot of conflict around Tait. Both Gloria Tyne and Kurt Boardman wanted to keep it relatively small and successful, but Mitchell Tait was determined to float the company on the stock exchange and enter the big league. I get the impression every attempt to argue against this course of action led to rather heated scenes. Anyway, he was getting his way…the arrangements for the float were in their final stages, though I imagine things will grind to a halt now."

"What's Kurt Boardman like?"

Bourke was highly amused. "You'll love him, Carol! If you could take the essence of everything that goes into high-powered selling and roll it up in one little package—it'd be Kurt Boardman."

Bourke was equally succinct about Gloria Tyne. "Moody, intense sort," he said, "who I suspect doesn't have a lot of close friends. Could hardly get a word out of her, though whether this is because she's broken-hearted or because she's just plain uncooperative, I don't really know. You might have more success with her."

Carol had a sudden thought. "Do you know which firm of stockbrokers is underwriting the shares?"

Bourke didn't, but would check. "You're thinking of John Brandstett, of course," he said. "I'll get back to you."

"Mark, I want to thank you—"

"Gosh, Carol, I haven't done anything yet. Thought I'd drop in one of my neat little tables with motives and opportunities all set out for you. *Then* you can thank me."

They chatted for a few moments, then, as Carol was about to say goodbye, Bourke said, "Learn anything this morning from Christine Tait?"

Her voice non-committal, Carol said, "Not really. Her alibi seems tight. Have you seen her yet?"

"I will in about half an hour. Seems she's recovered enough to face a gentle interrogation, as long as she has her legal representative on hand. Covering herself, isn't she?"

Carol kept the tartness out of her voice as she said, "She believes you think she and Brett Tait combined together to dispose of Mitchell."

Bourke laughed. "Does she? How perceptive of her!"

Christine was late. This was to be expected. She was always late. Carol walked around the house, peered through the glass into the room where Mitchell was killed, examined the area below the windows which Bourke had said was innocent of recent footprints, and took sightlines from different parts of the garden to discover what could be seen from outside. The extensive grounds had been landscaped for privacy, with high fences, strategically placed grassy banks and stands of native trees and bushes. It was an intruder's delight.

She strode around to the front where she had parked her car, impatient with anger that Christine should keep her waiting. Daylight saving had begun the weekend before, so it was still light at seven-thirty when Christine's blue BMW turned through the gates and came up the drive to park behind Carol.

Carol said sharply, "You're late."

Christine's smile was slow and warm. "Dearheart, you know I'm always a bit late."

The affectionate word stung. It had been three years since she had heard Christine call her that. Memories of the desolation she had felt when Christine ended their relationship made her savagely abrupt. "Come on, Chris, let's get it over with."

"It'll never be over, Carol."

Carol ignored the comment, striding towards the sandstone and slate entrance. "While I was waiting for you I checked the house and grounds. Everything looks okay, but I don't think it's a good idea for you to stay here by yourself."

Christine seemed nonchalant. "I'll be all right. I've

arranged for a security firm to check the grounds every few hours during the night and I'll switch the alarm on as soon as I'm alone."

"Chris, it could be someone you know. Not some anonymous intruder…someone you'd let into the house without a thought."

"I'll be careful. At least I'm safe with you here, aren't I?"

Carol followed her into the house, aware of everything about her: the way she moved, the turn of her head, her stillness as she stood at the doorway of each room and checked it out. She was wearing a simple blue dress, high-heeled backless sandals, a heavy silver bangle, but no wristwatch. Christine never wore a watch.

The interior had been left reasonably neat, but there was evidence everywhere of the twenty or so people who had examined every room with practiced eyes—cigarette ash, a piece of crumpled paper, a disposable cup that had held coffee left on a mantlepiece. Of course the scene of the murder had been painstakingly vacuumed for hair, fibers or any other microscopic evidence, but most surfaces still held traces of fingerprint powder.

The kitchen was large and designed for serious cooking. Christine was a gourmet cook and she had organized all the accoutrements of food preparation to an uncluttered plan that combined space with efficiency. As they entered the room, Christine stopped, puzzled. "My knives…" Above the main workbench a long wooden rack, obviously intended to hold a wide assortment of knives and other cutting implements, was empty.

In explanation, Carol said, "They've been taken for scientific examination, in case one's the murder weapon."

Christine looked appalled. "You mean someone might have washed it, and just put it back?" She bit her lip. "How horrible."

"You'll find they've taken some other things, too. Towels, clothes, shoes." Carol explained how drains were dismantled to check for human blood, remembering as she spoke that Bourke had said the kitchen sink had held traces. Who had stood there, thirty hours ago, washing Mitchell's blood away? She said, "Anything that might have been used or touched by the murderer has to be examined."

Christine shivered. "It's me! They're going to say it's me!"

"How can they? You were with Fiona Brandstett."

Christine put a hand over her mouth. "They'll twist things. When I saw Detective Bourke this afternoon I could tell what he was thinking...he kept asking me about Brett. He thinks the two of us did it. Doesn't he? Carol?"

"It doesn't matter what anyone thinks, it has to be proved and—"

"You will help me, won't you? Please?"

"You know I will. Just tell me the truth—all of it. For example, who is supposed to be framing you?"

"I don't know. I just sense there's someone trying to trap me. It's just a feeling, but I'm sure it's not my imagination."

"Do you have any enemies?"

Christine looked at her, sudden wry amusement trembling on her lips. "Of course I do! Every would-be society matron hates me if I don't serve on her committee."

Carol turned away in disgust. "If you're not going to be sensible..."

The laughter gone from her voice, Christine said, "Of course I'm going to be sensible. It's my neck, isn't it? Did Brett see you this afternoon? I asked him to."

Carol briefly summed up Brett's visit, including his avowal that there was nothing between himself and Christine.

"Dearheart, there *isn't*. Brett is a good friend. I can see why the police would like it if we were lovers—a perfect motive, isn't it? But it's not true. You do believe me, don't you?"

"Chris, you're sure there's nothing anyone can dig up?"

"Only that we're friends, good friends. And I've tried to help him. Mitchell was too hard on Brett...he refused to give him more money for the business, but I knew I could change his mind."

"Mitchell's will gives Brett a couple of hundred thousand."

Christine's tone was waspish. "Mitchell left *me* a lot more than that—so shouldn't I be the main suspect and Brett be left off the hook?"

"The reasoning would be that if you and Brett were lovers, he could reasonably expect to get his hands on your part of the estate as well."

Indignation widened Christine's eyes. "We're not lovers, Carol! We never have been and we never will be! You're the only lover I ever wanted!"

Anger, always there, spilled over. She said, "Don't, Chris."

Christine moved to put a hand on her arm. Carol was acutely aware of the curve of her lips. Christine said softly, "You can't know how much I've missed you..."

Shrugging off her touch, Carol said, "I don't need this, Chris. I don't want to be here. I never intended we'd ever meet again."

Christine's eyes were pleading. "Carol, you must understand! I was wrong. It was you, it was always you. I should never have stayed with Mitchell..."

"For God's sake, Chris! He's dead. Murdered. That's what's important, not what happened three years ago."

"What we had, you and I, we can have again."

"Forget it," said Carol harshly. "The past's gone and you've got quite enough to worry about in the present. I've said I'll help you, and I will, but don't—"

"Don't what?"

"Don't try to pretend there's still anything between us."

"But there is. You feel the way I do."

"The idea," said Carol coldly, "is to prevent you from being

48

charged with murder. Let's concentrate on that, shall we?"

Driving home, Carol cursed herself and Christine with equal vehemence. She had been able to stop the situation from escalating further by forcing Chris to discuss events rationally, taking her through her movements in detail for the whole day of the murder and establishing the strength of the alibi Fiona Brandstett provided her.

They had parted politely, Carol armed with a veneer of self-possession that hid her anger and precluded any deeper intimacy.

But none of that had prevented her body from betrayal. She yearned for Chris now, just as she had burned with desire for her so often before. But it was only a physical desire. Towards Chris she felt anger and resentment, but not love. Love had been a long time dying, but it had died.

And Sybil? What did she feel about Sybil? She had thought the affection growing between them was enough to build a firm relationship. But was it?

She made a resolve: I'll concentrate on the case. I'll concentrate on finding who killed Mitchell. *Then* I'll think about Sybil. And Chris…

She smiled without humor. Wasn't it the height of true romance to have not one, but *two* suitors?

It was after one o'clock when she swung into the street-level carport. She walked quietly down the path to find Sybil's Jeffrey and her Sinker sitting on either side of the front door studiously ignoring each other's presence. They were there, of course, to demand late supper. It was easier to provide it than put up with the cat version of guerilla warfare, so Carol opened a tin of fish and gave them a dish each. She turned out the lights and sat in the silver moonlight watching them eat, aware that she was postponing going to bed.

It was strange. Once she had longed to hear Chris say the words she had used tonight, "I was wrong...I should never have stayed with Mitchell..." Carol had imagined she might feel joy, or perhaps anger, if Chris ever made such a declaration, but what she did feel was a spiraling confusion that threatened the balance of her life.

When she finally went to bed Sybil turned sleepy arms to her.

Carol was afire. She felt the length of Sybil's slim body against her and gasped with the intensity of her desire.

Sybil, slowly awakening, responded to her urgent hands, opened her mouth beneath her seeking lips, matched her quickened breathing.

Carol wanted to drown in the erotic tide submerging her, to answer the imperative demands of her trembling body, to escape into sensation and forget everything else.

Sybil was fully awake now, caressing, holding, straining against her. Carol wanted to love her absolutely, to surrender herself, to merge. She murmured, "Darling, darling..." as her fingers slid, demanding, between Sybil's legs.

Sybil grew tight, tighter—was suddenly quivering with release, her breath hard against the hollow of Carol's neck. She relaxed suddenly, then her searching mouth began to devour Carol—sucking her nipples, sliding down her arching body, brushing the skin of her inner thighs...

Carol didn't want to call out—she wanted to keep the intensity of the feeling, to hide in the breathless ache that consumed her.

Sybil's mouth had found her center. She couldn't hold it any longer. Hips lifting, breath expelled in a wild cry, she surged to a climax, the rhythm going on and on until she was wet, exhausted and, impossibly, crying.

Sybil held her, rocking gently, silent in the darkness.

Chapter 4

Mark Bourke was as good as his word. Carol found a brown envelope slipped under the front door when she went, heavy-eyed, to see if the morning paper had been delivered. *Too early to wake you* was scribbled on the front.

Deciding to forgo her usual morning run, she flattened out the contents while she sipped a cup of strong black tea.

The first page was a detailed account of Mitchell Tait's last day. Nothing notable about his morning routine—he had risen early, made several telephone calls to business associates (all accounted for) before leaving for his North Sydney offices at seven forty-five. His arrival there was on schedule and his behavior was normal. At nine he held the regular weekly planning and assessment meeting with his partners, Kurt Boardman and Gloria Tyne. This meeting dealt with the usual day-to-day problems and issues and nothing unusual was discussed. Kurt Boardman left the meeting to go to the first of a series of sales calls. Gloria Tyne had remained discussing several technical issues with Mitchell until about ten, when they were interrupted by a call from his wife. It had been Mitchell's firm rule that no telephone calls were to intrude on any planning meeting, but his wife was exempted from this instruction and Mitchell's personal secretary had put Christine through immediately. Bourke had noted, *Mrs. Tait claims it was to remind him about a dinner date (to be checked out)*. Shortly afterwards, Brett Tait telephoned and waited until the line was clear before speaking to his brother. Gloria Tyne, who had come into the office especially for the planning session, left, saying she was going home to work on a computer program she was developing. This was not unusual, as she often avoided the interruptions and noise of the office in this way.

Just after ten-fifteen Tait had told his secretary, Rosie Lee, that he would be out of the office for a couple of hours and to reschedule any appointments he had for later in the afternoon. He gave no details of where he was going or if he would be meeting anyone, but his secretary did think he was preoccupied. He spoke to a couple of people about work-related matters and then left shortly afterwards without any other comment.

There was no firm sighting of him again, although one of the Taits' neighbors had volunteered a vague recollection of seeing Mitchell's car entering the driveway of the house. Bourke had written in pencil a wry comment: *Obviously the neighborhood busybody!* The time was uncertain, but probably just before eleven, which would indicate that he had driven straight home from the office. From that point on nobody had seen or heard or spoken to him, apart from his murderer.

Bourke had noted at the bottom of this sheet *So what did Mitchell Tait do in the two hours before he died?*

Carol frowned over the comment. She knew Mitchell's impatience and inability to relax. He always had to be involved or entertained. Many times she had seen him pace up and down, smoking, barely restraining his anger over a delay or because someone was late. Christine, with her habitual tardiness, had caused him endless irritation, although she was always serenely impervious to criticism on this account.

The second page was a photostat of one of Bourke's neat tables. It began with Christine's name, and Carol knew he had put the suspects in his personal descending order of likely guilt.

MITCHELL TAIT DIES WITHIN PERIOD
12:30 AM—1:30 PM WEDNESDAY

	OPPORTUNITY	POSSIBLE MOTIVES
Christine Tait	alibi from Fiona Brandstett — approx. 12— 1:45 PM	Brett Tait (lover?) Inheritance
Brett Tait	on road seeing clients lunch 12— 1 McDonald's Parra-matta (as yet no corroboration)	Christine Tait? Inheritance (needs cash urgently for business)
Gloria Tyne	working at home from 11:00 onwards (to be checked)	Mitchell Tait? (lover?) Control of company
Kurt Boardman	in and out all day seeing prospects (a possibility between appointments)	None apparent (stopping company going public too slight?)

| Fiona Brandstett | alibi (See Christine Tait above) | None apparent |
| John Brandstett | in his office until midafternoon (to be checked) | None apparent (some rumors of financial problems) |

Bourke had written in pencil at the bottom of the page, *Also checking out all Tait's business dealings. Should be some convincing motives there!*

The third item was a summary of the post mortem findings. She noted that Mitchell had not eaten breakfast, that he was showing early signs of arterial stenosis and that his lungs were discolored by heavy smoking. She skimmed through the details, stopping to re-read the clinical description of the dreadful injuries the knife had inflicted.

Carol sat, staring at nothing, thinking. Finally she stood and stretched, deciding to go for a run after all.

"Carol?"

She turned with a smile to Sybil. "Thought I'd let you sleep in."

Sybil was unsmiling, tense. "Last night, with Christine... what happened?"

"I checked out the house. We discussed Mitchell's death. That's all."

"You were home late."

"Yes."

Sybil's expression was remote. "I can't help feeling," she said, "that last night, when you came home, you were making love to *her*, not me."

"That isn't true."

Sybil moved to put her face against her shoulder. "Just my paranoia. Ignore it."

Carol put her arms around her, holding her tightly, saying to herself, *It isn't true…is it?*

She said, "Darling, I'm going for a run. Okay?"

A hug and she went to change, hungry for the solitude and the rhythm of her breathing to dispel the anxieties that rose chattering in her thoughts.

Rosie Lee, the pleasant middle-aged woman who had been Mitchell Tait's personal secretary, was visibly upset as she discussed with Carol the day he died. Christine had mentioned that Rosie Lee had been with Mitchell since well before the inception of TTB Computing and that he claimed he couldn't run an office without her. Rosie was a childless widow, the company had become a very important part of her life and she had watched with parental interest its growth from a tiny concern struggling to survive to its present success.

"Please excuse me," Rosie said several times as she dabbed at her eyes and blew her nose. She was a plump, fading blonde whose face still held traces of considerable beauty. Carol noticed that her dress, a quiet gray shade, was well-cut and her jewelry, though understated, was undeniably expensive.

Before asking any questions, Carol made sure Rosie understood that she was there unofficially.

Rosie nodded. "Mrs. Tait called this morning and explained you were a close friend. I'd be more than happy to do anything I could to find out who…" Her eyes filled with tears which she ineffectually brushed away. "I'm so sorry. I'll be all right in a moment."

Carol waited, sympathetic.

Rosie blew her nose again. "It's just Mitchell dying like that…"

"You've been with the company for some time, Ms. Lee?"

"Oh, yes. Since the beginning. In fact, I've been with Mitchell from well before he and Kurt and Gloria started TTB almost three years ago. I've seen it grow from one little room where we were all crammed together to this." She indicated with a movement of her head the slick office area around them.

TTB Computing's North Sydney premises were designed on an open plan so that the only divisions between the separate work stations and desks were low metal and glass partitions or strategically placed potted plants. The three partners had slightly more substantial offices situated along the wall of windows, placed to enjoy a spectacular view of Sydney city and the gray arch of Sydney Harbour Bridge. Carol and Rosie were sitting in Mitchell Tait's office and through the glass Carol could see the constant coming and going of employees and hear the hum of conversation, the click of computer keys, the insistent demands of telephones.

Twisting her sodden handkerchief in her fingers, Rosie said, "Mitchell was a good boss, Inspector. He could be hard, impatient, even difficult…but he was always fair to me. I loved working for him."

"On Wednesday, was he any different than usual?"

Rosie shook her head. "Not really. It was the weekly planning meeting. There's often a lot of tension then because Mitchell demands results. He's always been like that…"

"He didn't say or do anything you later thought was strange in any way?"

"No, not really. He was a bit preoccupied afterwards, as if he had something on his mind."

Rosie had taken minutes of all these Wednesday meetings, so she and Carol went through the items of the last meeting together, Rosie declaring that there was nothing out of place or unusual.

Carol said, "Tell me about Gloria Tyne and Kurt

Boardman."

Rosie's analysis paralleled, in most respects, what Carol already knew about Mitchell's two partners. Kurt Boardman was the quintessence of hard-sell, tenacious as a terrier when he saw an opportunity to push the company's software solutions; Gloria Tyne was a near-genius on the technical side and much of TTB Computing's success was due to her work in creating software packages.

Carol said, "Could you clarify for me how the partnership was set up?"

Mitchell Tait had gained wide experience in the computer industry by working for various companies. He had enjoyed considerable success, both professionally and financially, but had decided three years ago to start his own company on the strength of his entrepreneurial flair, Kurt Boardman's sales expertise and Gloria Tyne's technical abilities. Mitchell had raised the capital and, after a shaky start, the company had started to make money in a very competitive field, largely due to the superiority of its software products and the complementary skills of the three partners.

Carol said, "Wasn't there some conflict over whether or not the company should go public?"

Rosie nodded. "Yes, Mitchell was hellbent on getting into the sharemarket. He said it was the only way to get the necessary capital to really expand. Kurt and Gloria weren't keen...I think they wanted the company to stay small and manageable, but Mitchell wouldn't listen."

"Couldn't the two junior partners combine to outvote Mitchell?"

Rosie looked uncomfortable. "Well, yes—but in this case, although Gloria didn't really like the idea of going public, she sided with Mitchell against Kurt."

"Why would she do that?"

Rosie looked away. "I'm not sure," she said.

"Gloria Tyne is very upset about Mitchell Tait's death."

"We all are, of course."

Carol was at her most persuasive. "I know it's difficult—breaking confidences or seeming to gossip, but when someone has been murdered, things aren't the same. If you know something, please tell me."

Rosie looked at her with embarrassment clearly mirrored on her face. "At a time like this...to talk about Gloria and Mitchell..."

"They had a deeper relationship than just a working one?"

Rosie leaned back, apparently deciding how much to say.

Carol said, "Any details can be important, if only because of the light they may throw on other information. Please be frank."

Rosie made up her mind. She said, "All right. Gloria's a strange girl—she's very clever, very intense, doesn't relate well to other people. Mitchell took a personal interest in her, I don't know why, at first...but on Gloria's side I think it quickly became very, very important to her."

"How long ago was this?"

Rosie pursed her lips. "Six, maybe eight months ago. I could see Gloria was getting in over her head..."

"You said something?"

Rosie nodded wearily. "Yes, not that it did any good. Gloria was defensive and then nasty. Mitchell laughed it off at first, then he told me to mind my own business."

"So Gloria and Mitchell had an affair? Yes? And that's why she sided with him over the shares."

"I think so."

"Were Gloria and Mitchell still together when he died?"

Rosie looked at her in entreaty. "This will sound bad, but you mustn't put too much weight on it..."

"What happened?"

"I think it got too much for Mitchell—the scenes and the

intensity. He broke it off. Told Gloria it was over."

"How did she take this?"

Rosie sighed. "As well as you might expect—she was devastated."

"Devastated enough to consider killing him?"

"When you're that upset...you say things you don't mean..."

Carol was intrigued. After all her protestations, Rosie Lee was almost too forthcoming over the relationship between Gloria and Mitchell. Carol encouraged her with a tone of sympathetic interest. "Are you saying Gloria Tyne threatened Mitchell?"

Full of regret, Rosie said, "Only to me. I'm afraid she said she'd like to harm him, but I know it was only in the heat of the moment."

"What did she actually say?"

Rosie considered, then replied, "Gloria's exact words, as far as I can remember, were: *The bastard won't get away with it. I'll kill him first.*"

"Did you think she was serious?"

Rosie said, "At the time, but of course she would have cooled off later."

"When did Gloria make this threat?"

Rosie's expression became even more regretful. "Why," she said, "the day before Mitchell died."

Carol had time to study Kurt Boardman before he realized she was in his office. He was standing by the desk impatiently flicking through the pages of a manual, his freckled face set in a scowl of concentration. Short and somewhat stout, he hardly looked the prototype of the perfect salesperson, although he was impeccably dressed in an expensive gray suit and red tie.

Balding, he had painstakingly combed the surviving sandy strands across the bare areas.

Carol cleared her throat and he looked up immediately. The transformation was astonishing. His scowl changed to a warm, welcoming smile and he strode to meet Carol, hand extended.

"Detective Inspector Ashton, it is a pleasure to meet you. I've followed those cases of yours with admiration."

Carol was amused to find herself on the verge of thanking him for his interest in her career. Instead she said, "Mrs. Tait was to ring you and explain that my position here is entirely unofficial."

"Indeed, Christine did call me. She said you'd been friends for years."

There was a sting in his remark that he didn't intend, that Carol felt with a keenness that disconcerted her. Friends with Chris? How could the depth of what they had once had ever be described as friendship?

Kurt ushered Carol into a chair and retreated behind his desk, which was large, highly polished and graced by a black onyx desk set of ostentatious design.

Carol thought, I bet he drives a Porsche. She couldn't resist. "Do you drive a Porsche?"

He smiled at her in self-mockery. "Of course I do," he said, "I'm a successful salesman, aren't I?"

She had to laugh. "I deserved that. I'm sorry."

As Carol began to question him, it became obvious why Kurt Boardman was so good at his job. He watched her with close attention, considered her words, answered with sincerity. The impression he gave was of a person who was warm, truthful and helpful. Christine had told her Kurt had been recently divorced, apparently by mutual consent and without animosity. She wondered what he thought of Mitchell, so conspicuously successful in business and in his personal life.

Carol said, "Can you think of anyone who would like Mitchell Tait dead?"

For the first time Kurt's attention wavered. He began to play with a glossy executive toy consisting of curved chrome wires swinging in complicated arcs. He said, "Mitchell wanted to go public with TTB Computing. It's no secret I opposed the move, but he was adamant because he thought we needed the capital. John Brandstett's stockbroking company was going to underwrite the shares, but just recently Mitchell told me he'd discovered not only was John involved in some rather shady dealings, but Brandstett and Nicholls itself was quite shaky financially."

"You're suggesting John Brandstett had a motive?"

"Mitchell could be formidable if anything went wrong. When he realized the situation, he threatened John—told him he'd go to the authorities and have his company investigated. I talked to Mitchell about it, and not only was he angry he'd been made a fool of, he was furious about the delay to the share float, since he'd have to find another underwriter."

"You were against the company going public anyway, weren't you?"

"That's no secret, but I certainly wasn't going to kill Mitchell over it. Besides, this delay meant I'd have a chance to persuade Mitchell to hold off." He smiled self-deprecatingly. "I'm a very persuasive person when I try," he said.

"Regarding John Brandstett, was the situation you describe desperate enough for him to seriously consider harming Mitchell?"

Kurt leaned forward to sell the idea. "Mitchell was very influential, Inspector Ashton. He had wide experience both in the computer field and in business generally. And he knew the key people. All he needed to do was to drop a few words in the right places and John Brandstett was in deep, deep trouble."

Carol said, "I understand Brandstett's secretary says he was in his office at the time of the murder."

"Well, there you are. Can't be John Brandstett, can it?"

Carol raised an eyebrow at his tone. "Do you have any reason to think that isn't true?"

"No. Only that Mitchell told me he intended to see Brandstett the day he died."

"Have you mentioned this before?"

Kurt shrugged. "No, it wasn't important enough. As far as I know there wasn't a firm appointment. Mitchell said he would telephone Brandstett and set up a meeting. That's all I know. And since Brandstett's secretary says he was safely in his office in the city, I suppose he has an alibi."

"Speaking of alibis," said Carol pleasantly, "I believe you were seeing clients when Mitchell was killed."

He nodded briskly. "The police have my appointment diary, although you should know that I can't account for every minute. I'm quite aware it might have been possible for me to squeeze in a visit to Lindfield...although I didn't."

Carol was curious. "Do you know Mitchell's time of death?"

He gave her a tight smile. "Of course not, but I *do* know the period the police are showing an unhealthy interest in, so I'd say Mitchell was killed somewhere between half past twelve and half past one." He looked at her interrogatively. "Well? How's that for an educated guess?"

Pretty good, thought Carol. Aloud she said, "I'm not altogether sure of the time."

Kurt Boardman shook her hand again as she left his office. His fingers were dry and smooth and his grip nicely firm, reassuring and not too prolonged. Carol looked back at him as he walked to his desk smoothing his sandy hair carefully across his scalp. He *seemed* open, sincere and helpful—but didn't all successful sales people? And, in the same way Rosie Lee was selling Gloria Tyne as a principal suspect, Kurt was pushing John Brandstett.

If Kurt Boardman had been welcoming, Gloria Tyne was working to create the opposite impression. She looked up frowning as Carol knocked on the half-open door and snapped, "Yes? What do you want?"

As Carol introduced herself, she observed Gloria Tyne closely. Her clothes, a blouse and skirt, looked as though she had thrown them on unironed, and she wore no jewelry, not even a watch. She had wildly untamed hair of a caramel color, dark eyes so swollen they almost looked bruised, and a tight rosebud mouth. Her fingernails were bitten and her hands stained with nicotine. She tapped the end of a cigarette with nervous jabs against the desk as she listened to Carol's explanation of who she was and why she was here.

"Christine Tait rang me," Gloria said abruptly. "I know who you are. Sorry I can't help you."

As Carol sat down, uninvited, she said sympathetically, "You must be very upset at what's happened."

Gloria lit the cigarette, sucked fiercely and blew a stream of angry smoke in Carol's direction. Her expression was one of sullen grief, but her tone was sharp. "So I'm upset. So what?"

Carol decided to go for the jugular. "I'm told you had a very close personal relationship with Mitchell."

"Oh? I suppose Rosie told you that? Bloody busybody."

Carol's tone remained mild. "Is it true that he broke it off with you?"

"No!"

"That's what I've been told."

Gloria sprang to her feet and began to stride about the office. There was a kind of desperate loneliness about her that touched Carol, so that she said, "I'm sorry to upset you."

Gloria whirled on her. "Sorry? What does it matter? He's dead."

"Do you have any idea who could have done it?"

"Idea?" said Gloria bitterly. "I *know*. It was that bitch, his wife. Christine, she killed him. It was Christine."

Chapter 5

"It's all too hard, Carol...I love you but I just can't give up everything. I can't leave Mitchell. It's over...you do understand, don't you?"

The words, so often remembered, were singing in Carol's head, their power to hurt revitalized.

She jogged steadily along the bush path in the cool of the early Saturday morning, her neighbor's German Shepherd, Olga, loping beside her. The wiry gray-green shrubs of the Australian bush crowded the dirt track, with dashes of sudden color where wildflowers grew tenaciously in the inhospitable sandy soil. Overhead the branches of the gumtrees were alive with birds building nests, quarreling over mates, looking for food along the path that wound along the edge of the innumerable little bays of the upper harbor.

It was a punishing route through the huge harborside nature reserve, but Carol hardly noticed the tightness of her chest or the ache in her legs. Memories crowded her thoughts. A few made her smile; others were corrosive. In all her adult life, only three events had made her cry unrestrainedly: the death of her mother; giving up her son; Christine telling her it was all over.

The very first time she had seen Christine had been a searing summer's morning, breathless with the stored heat of a series of brassy days. Justin had insisted that she come to the luncheon Mitchell and Christine Tait were holding, a casual barbecue around the pool of their new house in Lindfield. It was important for Justin to be there, complete with attractive wife—Mitchell Tait was an up-and-coming businessman, Christine Tait came from the influential Shadforth family, their friends were the people whose good favor would materially help Justin Hart's promising career in the law.

Even then, Carol and Justin had led essentially separate lives. Their marriage had grown into a genial coexistence, each of them absorbed in a demanding career, but held together by mutual respect and by their love for David, who had then been a chubby, gravely inquisitive four-year-old.

Justin had insisted she wear a crisp green casual dress to complement what he called the startling jade of her eyes. She had been reluctant to leave her work, but, as the luncheon was important to him, she complied. Sometimes afterwards she would wonder what would have happened had she not gone… But of course she would have met Christine somewhere else, at some other time.

She could still remember the extraordinary impact Christine had had upon her that day. They had been introduced and Christine had smiled at her, that slow, lazy smile Carol later knew so intimately. She had begun to feel an excited discomfort, a strange and unsettling longing she had never experienced before.

Christine was wearing a simple white dress that swirled as she turned. Carol couldn't remember what they talked about. Whatever it was, it was fractured by the constant demands of guests and hospitality, but she knew that Christine was seeking her out, making opportunities to exchange a few words.

Ironically, Justin had been extremely pleased that she had got on so well with Christine. "It would be useful to have the Taits as friends," he said pragmatically.

Carol had done her best to disregard the disturbing fascination Christine Tait had created, deliberately turning her thoughts away from the vivid impression of her perfume, the heavy silver bracelet on her slim wrist, the sound of her throaty laugh.

The next time was easier. Carol was prepared for her feelings and so could keep them in check. Always, she had known she felt an attraction towards some women. It was never allowed to become important—just acknowledged and then ignored. But with each succeeding meeting what she was feeling became harder and harder to disregard.

She and Justin had become warmly accepted friends of the Taits. Justin, delighted, took every opportunity to build the relationship between the couples. Carol's career was demanding and she often found genuine excuses to avoid seeing the Taits, but even so, more and more she found herself in Christine's company.

One hot Wednesday morning almost a year after they had first met, Christine called her to suggest a swim in her pool. Carol had taken a few days leave after a particularly trying case, David was at school, so there was no reason to refuse the invitation.

Christine met her at the door. "Carol, there's something I must talk to you about." She took her through to the kitchen, offered her coffee, then leaned forward and kissed her on the mouth.

After all this time Carol could still remember the surge of shocked desire that filled her. Christine, smiling, had said, "I've wanted to do that for so long."

"What do I say?"

Christine laughed. "Say that you love me. You do, don't you?"

"This is impossible."

"Dearheart, of course it isn't!"

And then it began—the headlong descent into a passionate love affair that would eventually end in disaster.

The first time they made love Carol realized that whatever had passed for it before in her experience was a pale shadow of the real thing. She was filled with emotions so deep, desires so strong, that the foundations of her ordered life were shaken and, ultimately, destroyed.

Pictures whirled in a kaleidoscope of impressions: Justin's face when she told him she was leaving him and why; Christine's promises to join her soon; Carol's unthinking conviction that David would remain with her; Justin's threats and legal influence combined with Christine's pleas not to make a scandal that eventually persuaded her to give David up; and then, at the last, Christine's white face and final determined words as she told Carol it was all too hard and that their relationship was over.

Carol was returned to the present by the pain of her laboring lungs. Unconsciously she had been quickening her pace so that now the breath was sobbing in her throat. Even Olga, pink tongue lolling, was panting hard beside her. Carol slowed to a walk.

She said, "No, Chris…not again. Not ever again."

Sybil frowned as she went to answer the doorbell. Who would be calling this early in the morning?

"Excuse me. I'm Christine Tait. Is Carol in?"

"She's out running. She shouldn't be long."

Christine smiled. "I'm sorry, I don't know your name."

Sybil gave a careful smile in return. She said, "Sybil. Sybil Quade. Would you like to come in?"

Following her down the hall, Sybil was suspended in an absorption of every detail of the woman Carol had loved— might still love.

Christine wasn't as tall as Sybil had thought but she moved with a grace she hadn't suspected either. Her honey-blonde hair had a smooth understated elegance that her own red curls could never attain; her white jeans and mauve silk shirt were worn with effortless style; her simple silver bracelet was just enough to complete the effect. Christine seemed fully as fascinated by Sybil as Sybil was by her, and it was with a mutual cool amusement that they viewed each other.

Christine accepted a mug of coffee and looked speculatively over the rim as she drank. Then she said, "You were leaving on Thursday for an overseas holiday with Carol, weren't you? I'm sorry—I'm the reason you didn't go."

Sybil nodded politely. Christine had a low voice, husky and confiding.

Christine said, "Have you known Carol long?"

"Not really. Less than a year."

Christine slid her eyes away, took in the room. She said conversationally, "Carol moved in here after her parents died. Of course, you wouldn't have known them…"

"No."

Anger began to tighten Sybil's jaw. She was very conscious that Christine was playing the I-know-more-about-her-than-you game, and she was determined not to be drawn in. She said, "I'm sure Carol won't be long."

Christine was looking directly at her again, frowning slightly. "We've never met, have we? I feel I've seen your face before."

"We've never met," said Sybil unhelpfully.

They both heard Carol's footsteps on the polished wood of the hall. She came into the room, then stopped abruptly when she saw Christine.

Sybil couldn't bear to see the expression that might be on Carol's face, so she turned away, murmured an apology and left them together. Savage with resentful anger, she grabbed her car keys and strode out of the house with no idea where she might go, but with the firm conviction that she had to be somewhere else.

"Why are you here, Chris?"

"Are you angry I came?"

Carol sat down and began to unlace her running shoes, her head turned from Christine so that her straight blonde hair fell to cover her face.

Christine knelt, her hand stilling Carol's fingers at the laces. She said, "I can't bear it when you're angry with me."

"Were you curious about Sybil, or is it something else?"

Christine laughed, stood up, slid onto a tall stool at the breakfast bench. "You know me so well, Carol. It wasn't the only reason, but I admit I wanted to meet the owner of that delightful voice on the telephone. I'm sure I've seen her before somewhere…"

"Sybil was involved in a murder case at the beginning of the year. There was a lot of publicity."

"Of course—I remember. The Premier's son, right?" When Carol didn't respond, she said, "She's quite beautiful, isn't she? And that red hair—"

70

Carol interrupted. "Look, Chris, I'm not going to discuss Sybil with you."

Christine became grave. "Is it serious?"

"Yes."

Letting her breath out in a long sigh, Christine said, "I see."

There was a pause, broken as Carol stood up abruptly, running shoes in one hand. "What was the other reason you came?"

"Gloria Tyne's threatened me."

"How?"

"She rang me early this morning, practically incoherent—said she knew I'd killed Mitchell—said she'd do anything to make sure I paid for it."

"Meaning?"

Christine grimaced. "Meaning she wants revenge. I suppose you know about her affair with Mitchell? Well, when she turned out to be far too intense and erratic for him to comfortably handle, Mitchell tried getting rid of her by saying I'd found out and had given him an ultimatum—either give up Gloria or watch the business go down the drain."

"Could you do that? Ruin the business?"

"I could make things difficult I suppose—the usual joint settlement after divorce would take a lot of capital out of the company."

Carol sat down, putting her running shoes to one side and sinking back to watch Christine closely. Their eyes met and Christine gave her a slow smile. "It's wonderful to be with you again."

Carol disregarded the comment, saying, "Had you given him that ultimatum?"

"Hardly. At the time I didn't even know Mitchell and Gloria were an item."

"But you knew later?"

Christine was sardonically amused. "I had to know. Gloria, believing every word Mitchell said, started a campaign of telephone calls and threats to me...she was quite irrational. What complicated things was that Mitchell wanted me to treat Gloria with kid gloves because the company depends so much on her technical abilities. She's literally irreplaceable, and she knows it."

Carol said casually, "How did you feel about the affair, when you found out?"

"To be honest, I suppose I was irritated."

"Is that all?"

Christine looked at her earnestly. "I didn't *love* him, Carol. Of course there was some feeling between us, but Mitchell and I didn't have the kind of relationship that's based on jealousy."

Carol's face grew hard. "That isn't true. I know—first hand."

Christine moved to take Carol's hand. "Oh, he was jealous of *you*, but that's because I really cared. I still do."

Carol shook her fingers off. "When Mitchell died—what was the situation with Gloria Tyne?"

"She'd convinced herself that *I* was the only thing that stood between her and bliss with Mitchell," said Christine flippantly. "I was sick of the whole situation, so I told Mitchell to tell Gloria *he* wanted to end the affair and it was nothing to do with me."

"Did he tell her?"

Christine shrugged. "I don't know. If he did, she was so unpredictable..."

"Are you suggesting Gloria killed him?"

Christine threw her hands up. "Yes, maybe...I don't know." She put a hand on Carol's shoulder. "But I do know she'd be delighted to see *me* accused of murder. She hates me, really hates me."

Carol thought of Gloria Tyne's last words to her: "It was

that bitch, his wife. Christine, she killed him."

She said, "Chris, sit down. I want to talk to you about Gloria and Kurt Boardman—and also, Rosie Lee."

"Rosie Lee?" said Christine, puzzled. "What's Rosie Lee got to do with it?"

"I'm not sure…but there's a false note there."

Later in the day, when Carol telephoned Bourke, he was intrigued and amused by her questions. "Rosie Lee?" he said, "Don't tell me I've missed a warm passion swelling in that ample breast!"

"If you're suggesting Rosie Lee was in love with Mitchell, I don't know about that, but she certainly is doing her best to make sure Gloria falls under suspicion. I suppose it could be jealousy."

"What other reason would she have to shaft Gloria Tyne?"

"I was rather hoping you might find that out, Mark."

Bourke laughed. "Your wish, as always, is my command. Have you got anything else for me?"

Carol briefly recounted the information Christine had given her about Gloria's threats to her and how Mitchell had agreed to tell Gloria the truth.

"Right! That's interesting, Carol. Gloria Tyne might be off the planet, but she's sharp enough to recognize what might give her a motive for murder. She didn't breathe a word about Christine Tait, but left the firm impression she was happy to continue a low-key affair with Mitchell ad infinitum."

"Not what Rosie Lee says."

Bourke sounded dubious. "Rather convenient for Gloria to threaten to kill him the day before he died. Seems to me very stupid to go ahead and stab Tait within twenty-four hours of happily incriminating yourself."

"Swept away by passion?" said Carol ironically.

"Don't think so, Carol. This one was definitely premeditated. Not one of the knives we took from the house has any sign of human blood and no knives are missing. Whatever was used to stab Mitchell Tait was taken there, used, then taken away. And it was a substantial size, somewhere in the order of twenty or so centimeters—say, ten inches. Something like a large chefs knife with a broad blade and one sharp cutting edge tapering to a sharp point. Not the sort of thing Gloria Tyne would usually carry in her handbag along with her makeup."

They discussed the weapon further, then Bourke said, "By the way, you might be interested to know that I interviewed Fiona Brandstett again, and during our little chat she did manage to drop the comment that she thought Brett was, as she put it, 'rather recklessly over-emotional' about his brother's wife."

"Did she mean they were lovers?"

"Gosh, no, Carol! She was very careful to suggest that Christine had made it clear to Brett that all his adoration was to come from afar."

"What are you thinking, Mark?"

"I'm thinking," said Bourke, "that Fiona could be indulging in an attempt at damage control on Christine Tait's behalf. It's too dangerous to admit Brett and Christine are having an affair because a motive for her husband's death immediately leaps to mind. So much better to make it clear that Brett's love is unrequited."

Carol said, her skepticism clear, "Mark, this is too farfetched. You don't even have evidence that Brett and Christine are particularly close."

The satisfaction was evident in Bourke's voice. "I certainly do. When we searched the place after the murder the contents of Tait's desk were taken in for examination. I was looking for some financial problem, something to do with the business, that kind of thing. Anyway, there was a letter, most definitely of the love variety, from Brett to Christine."

Carol was silent. You've lied to me, Chris, she thought.

Bourke said, "Carol?"

"Yes, go on."

"Thought I'd spring it on them first thing Monday morning after I have an expert check the handwriting to make sure it's genuine."

She said evenly, "Why the trouble of handwriting analysis at this stage?"

Bourke's voice held the amused tone that always went with his delight in a challenging puzzle. "I hate to be over-suspicious," he said, "but I get the impression there are enough red herrings being thrown around to keep a Russian cannery busy, so I want to make absolutely sure every bit of evidence is on the up and up. You have to admit accusations are flying thick and fast. Rosie Lee wants us to think it's the intense Gloria Tyne; Gloria Tyne, in turn, accuses Christine Tait; Kurt Boardman is determined to shaft John Brandstett; Fiona Brandstett hints, ever so obliquely, that Brett Tait has blood on his hands. It's probably only a matter of time before Christine says it's Santa Claus."

They made arrangements for Carol to collect a copy of the letter found in Mitchell's deask and then they spent some time discussing the scientific analysis of murder scene and the post mortem report.

"It would take guts, but a woman could do it," said Bourke. "The entry point is central, just under the diaphragm— probably right-handed, but not definitely so—the blade was forced upwards and twisted. There was an absolute intention to kill…not just to wound."

"Is anyone left-handed?"

"Rosie Lee is."

Carol said dryly, "Rosie Lee has been elevated to suspect? She wasn't on your list."

"These days I play it s safe—I wouldn't want to be accused of sexism as far as suspects are concerned. And speaking of women, I wonder if you'd be interested in trying to shake the Christine-Fiona alibi a little. Bringing my famous lateral thinking to bear, I've begun to wonder if it could be *Christine* who's giving Fiona the alibi, and not the otherway round."

Carol thought, What could possibly persuade Chris to give Fiona an alibi?

She said, "Has Fiona a strong motive?"

"If the information I've been given is accurate, John Brandstett and his company are teetering on the edge of total collapse and Mitchell Tait was just about to knock the props out from under and bring the whole lot down. Fiona doesn't strike me as a woman who'd take to poverty, let alone disgrace, with any enthusiasm. Gives both Fiona and her husband quite a respectable motive, don't you agree?"

"It's a thought," said Carol, "but what about Brandstett's partner, Nicholls?"

"Long gone—Brandstett bought him out some years ago before the big stock market downturn shook the guts out of the company. Brandstett's kept up appearances since, but the business is slowly bleeding to death. He was relying on a transfusion from Tait, but our Mitchell pulled the tube out."

It was a relief to laugh. "Mark, you put things so soberly! Why don't you put some sparkle into your conversation?"

Fiona Brandstett's telephone manner was terse. "See you?" she repeated with frosty surprise.

Carol's polite insistence finally won a guarded concession. "But only for a few minutes."

Driving to the Brandstett place at Darling Point, Carol reviewed the questions she wanted to ask. She knew from Christine that Fiona was doing everything possible to help with the arrangements for a funeral that the media would attend with intrusive enthusiasm. Carol had been puzzled by the depth of friendship between Christine and Fiona Brandstett. Obviously it had social advantages for both of them, but there seemed to be something more than that, now that it was put to the test. She was surprised that Fiona had rallied to the cause when the publicity had hit the media. She would have expected a graceful, regretful withdrawal, but Fiona was still actively seeking Christine's company, reporters or no reporters. If Bourke's theory on the alibi had any weight, the reason for Fiona's devotion could be linked to self-preservation.

Fiona, a hint of haughty superiority in her bearing, met Carol at the door with an insecure quarter-power smile. "Any help I can be…" she murmured as she ushered Carol into the main room which was bright with reflected metallic light. Her tone indicated that she doubted she could offer any assistance.

Carol had dressed carefully in a light beige linen suit. She wanted Fiona to relax and talk freely, and she hoped the right image—one of careful taste—might help.

"I can't imagine why you need to see me again."

Carol said blandly, "Christine and I have been friends for some time…"

A shade of emotion flickered for a moment on Fiona's face. "Please don't bother to be indirect. I'm quite aware of the relationship you had with Christine."

Carol didn't miss the slight emphasis on "had." She said, mildly, "It was over three years ago. Chris has asked me to help her as a friend, nothing more."

"For Christine's sake I am quite willing to cooperate fully with you, but I fail to see what I can do or say that will be of any help at all."

Opting for an air of shared confidentiality, Carol leaned forward. "I'm sure you realize the alibi you've given Christine saves her from being the main suspect for her husband's murder. For that reason, it's important for the police to test it—to make sure it's as firm as it appears."

"It is," said Fiona patronizingly.

"You're absolutely sure Christine was with you continuously from just after noon until shortly before two? Is there any way you could be mistaken or confused?"

"This is a waste of time. I've been over it a hundred times."

"It's vital for Chris that it stand up to investigation. And for you, too, of course."

Raising her eyebrows, Fiona said, "For me? I'm not involved in this. I had no possible reason to harm Mitchell."

"Would you describe yourself as a friend of his?"

Fiona's mouth tightened. "John and I were close personal friends of both the Taits."

"So your own relationship with Mitchell was a good one?"

"Yes."

"Even though your husband's business dealings with him were the source of some friction?"

Fiona looked politely bored. "Business matters had nothing to do with our friendship with Christine and Mitchell."

"Were you aware that your husband and Mitchell had had several heated arguments?"

"John handles the business side of things. I have no interest in it. Now, if that's all…"

You think you're in control, thought Carol, but maybe I can shake your composure just a little. "I think Brett Tait is about to involve Christine—"

Fiona exclaimed, "Brett! He can't be relied on to tell the truth."

"No?"

"Certainly not where Christine is concerned."

"It seems to me he has a very real affection for her."

Fiona's contempt was directed both at Carol and at the absent Brett. "If possible," she said coldly, "I am even less interested in your opinions of Brett than I am in Brett Tait himself. He's emotionally immature and capable of lying when it suits him. Whatever he may say about Christine should never be taken at face value." She paused, then continued, "Brett imagines himself in love with Christine, that much is clear. I don't believe he's entirely rational about it…" Her expression indicated that murder was but one of the courses of action Brett might conceivably be expected to take.

Carol pressed gently. "Christine is very fond of her brother-in-law…"

"If you're trying to imply that they are lovers, you're wasting your time. Christine had a friendly interest in Brett, that's all. Surely she's told you this herself. You don't need to hear it secondhand from me."

Carol said, "Does Brett like you?"

Fiona blinked at the unexpected question. "Does Brett like me? He has no reason to feel one way or the other. Why? What has he said?"

Intrigued at the urgency under Fiona's disdainful tone, Carol showed a moderate surprise. "What would he say?"

Fiona obviously wanted to get off the subject. "I've no idea. Now, if you don't mind…"

Ignoring the cue, Carol persisted, "Perhaps he felt you were antagonistic towards him."

Fiona stood, brushing the creases from her classically cut skirt. "I am sorry," she said, "but I do have another appointment…"

Carol smiled. "Of course," she said, "and thank you for your help."

She had the impression that Fiona would stand, staring at the door, long after she had gone.

Chapter 6

On Sunday Carol made a resolute effort to put everything to do with Mitchell's murder out of her mind. She picked up David early and took him back to Seaforth to collect a picnic lunch and board her little cabin cruiser moored at the foot of the slope.

David had all the bubbling enthusiasm of a nine-year-old, and was bursting with news of the computer his father had just bought him. Carol felt a cold shaft of jealous regret that she could not be involved in the day-to-day events of her son's life, but had to be content with a peripheral role.

David was very like her. She smiled at his eager face and his green eyes smiled back. His hair was so blond it was almost white and his skin, like hers, tanned easily to a golden brown.

As Carol watched him steer the boat with more zest than

skill, she unwillingly remembered all the steps, all the agonies, all the tears, that had led to giving up custody of her son. If it were to happen now she knew she never would be persuaded, but then, three years ago, it had seemed best for David. And who was to say it wasn't? He adored his father, his stepmother was a warm and loving woman and Carol was able to see him whenever she wished without restrictions or recriminations.

They spent the day puttering around Middle Harbour, exploring little inlets and scrambling ashore at several points to explore. Every now and then David demanded they stop so he could try out the fishing rod Carol had given him for his birthday. He was disappointed Sybil wasn't there—he had promised to teach her how to fish—but he used Carol as a substitute, explaining in great detail how to cast the line. When he finally caught a wriggling light brown flathead, he made her watch closely as he lectured on how to remove the hook and avoid the sharp dorsal fins.

Carol, delighted though she was to have David to herself for a day, felt Sybil's absence more keenly than she had expected. Once Sybil's habitual reserve was breached, she was a delightful companion, having a warm, wry sense of humor and a wholehearted enjoyment in new experiences. She had a particularly infectious laugh that made others involuntarily smile and as she had relaxed more and more in Carol's company her amused comments had been both entertaining and endearing.

But in the last few days a subtle change had come over their relationship, and Christine's unannounced arrival yesterday had accelerated the process. Sybil had, in many ways, reverted to the restrained, reserved woman she had first met. There was still the same warm humor, but it was infrequent and careful. And Carol had found herself looking up and catching Sybil watching her, as though Sybil was waiting for something to happen or something to be resolved. Between them, as tangible as though she stood there, was Christine.

Last night Sybil, her jaw firm with resolution, had said, "Did you have any idea Christine would call here this morning?"

"No, of course not." Carol had hesitated and then added, "I think she was curious about you."

"Oh? And how do I shape up? Serious competition?"

The bitterness in Sybil's voice made Carol flinch. She said, "It's not like that."

Sybil didn't respond, but looked at her steadily until Carol felt compelled to add, "Chris is turning to me because she's frightened."

"What do you feel about her...now?"

Carol had wondered how she would answer that question when Sybil asked it. Last night, she had said, reluctantly, "I'd be lying if I said I felt nothing...

I know I'm angry..." Meeting Sybil's watchful eyes, she finished, lamely, "I don't really know."

Sybil's mouth tightened. In the aching silence Carol tried to think of something to say, something that would make everything right again, but could find no words to fit.

Sybil said, "I'm just a spectator, waiting for something to happen. I can't say or do anything to resolve the situation between you and Christine."

"It will be over soon."

"So you keep saying."

Carol said, with more conviction than she felt, "We'll leave for Europe as soon as Mark makes an arrest."

"Carol, you realize if she's guilty...you could be dragged into it. The affair you had with her could become public knowledge."

"Chris didn't kill Mitchell."

"She could still be accused of it."

Carol had shrugged, deliberately offhand. "I'll worry about that if it happens."

"Fine, Carol. But what about me?"

Now, sitting in the little launch, rocking gently in the lazy swell, Carol watched David bait his hook and allowed herself to fully consider the issue Sybil had raised. Would it be possible to avoid public exposure as a lesbian if the unthinkable happened and Christine went to trial? Her vivid imagination conjured up a worst case scenario—Christine indicted for murder, herself called as a witness. Surely the prosecution would be tempted to use the information that they had been lovers as a reflection of Christine's morality. The defense could have another reason—the suggestion that Carol, discarded by Christine three years before, had now seized the opportunity for revenge.

She had been involved in so many murder trials that she could easily picture herself in the witness box, the relentless questions, the admissions she would have to make. And the media…Carol's high profile would guarantee sensational coverage. What would that do to David? To Sybil? To her own career?

Her thoughts were interrupted by David's joyful exclamation as he caught another fish. As she showed the required interest and admiration over his accomplishment she pushed the images away. Chris was innocent. The issue of public exposure of her own private life was something she wouldn't have to face—at least, not now.

Sybil had said she was spending the whole day with friends, but when Carol returned from taking David home with his prized two-fish catch she was sitting on the back deck waiting, her back straight with tension. As Carol approached, Sybil rose and stood watching her soberly.

The deck was bathed in late afternoon light and filled with

the sound of humming life from the bush that crowded around in all its harsh beauty. Ordinarily they would have enjoyed a drink and a chat about the day. The awkwardness between them now hurt Carol with pain of an intensity that surprised her. She said, "We have to talk."

Sybil was calmly businesslike. "Carol, this is crazy. I'm so angry about the situation, about Christine. I think it's best if I move out—"

"No."

Sybil smiled briefly. "How reassuringly emphatic!"

"Darling…"

"Do you call her darling, too?"

At Carol's grimace of protest she shook her head ruefully. "Sorry, that was a cheap shot. I'm just not coping very well. I know I'm probably over-reacting to the whole situation."

"There isn't a situation." Carol put her arms around her and they stood quietly together. Carol's tight throat made her voice husky as she said, "I care about you. I—"

Sybil stepped back abruptly, breaking the embrace. "Are you going to say you love me? Don't tell me you love me! Don't tell me that!"

She turned, rejecting Carol with a gesture, and went into the house. Following her, Carol was startled, and then aroused, by the electricity of Sybil's sudden anger. She seized Sybil's shoulder, turned her until they stood face to face.

Her voice vibrating with rage, Sybil said, "You have such power over me, Carol! I need you so much…"

Their mouths met in a kiss so passionate that Sybil broke away, breathless, saying with angry humor, "You're addictive, Carol—you should be banned."

Her body singing, ringing with desire, Carol said, "Darling, please…"

At first Sybil resisted, but then, abruptly she capitulated, sliding with Carol to the bright rug on the polished wooden floor. They knew each other so well now, knew the triggers and the pleasures, knew how to prolong the breathless longing to peak intensity, but they had never made love like this before. Sybil had always held something in reserve—a still, private part of herself that nothing could touch or disturb. Now, she abandoned all restraint both in giving and receiving.

She teased Carol's nipples with her tongue and teeth, at one moment rough, then with melting gentleness, her hands sliding, touching, plunging—sometimes with feather softness, sometimes with urgent firmness. And in turn, Carol, her body taut, felt, smelled, heard Sybil's passion breaking like a continuous wave until they both were shaken by the rhythms of release.

Wet with sweat, her pulse hammering in her ears, Carol said the words she had so often avoided. "I love you."

Sybil laughed, breathless, refusing to take her seriously, "That's just the sex talking."

Carol felt the moment, the opportunity, slipping away. She couldn't say it again, and mean it, really mean it. She turned her face to Sybil's naked shoulder, tasted the salt and was silent.

Monday morning had an edge to it, a feeling of inevitability. Early, even before Carol had left for her run, Brett Tait had called. "Sorry it's so early, but I must see you."

Driving to his apartment, Carol thought of Sybil, and of Christine. Disconnected fragments of conversations, sudden snapshots of frozen memories, circled warily in her mind. She tried to use the logical precision she brought to her work: isolate the problems, examine the alternatives, make a decision. It wouldn't work—her thoughts were out of focus, twisting and turning when she tried to control them, then stabbing her with unexpected pain when she least expected it.

Brett met her at the door with nervous impatience, his little boy look fraying at the edges. He no longer lived in the smart apartment she remembered from the past, but had moved to a battered weatherboard house which had been divided into two dingy flats. Brett had always found it important to have the best, so this drop in standards made it clear that he was finding times hard.

He didn't stand on ceremony. Hardly waiting until she was seated on an overstuffed ancient sofa of hideous design, he said, "Are they going to arrest me?"

Carol raised her eyebrows. "What makes you think they might?"

"Carol, you'd know, wouldn't you, if they were going to?"

She frowned at the urgency in his voice. "Has something happened?"

Brett pushed the hair out of his eyes. "I wanted to see Chris yesterday—I needed to see her—but she said no."

Carol felt her impatience bubbling. "What's the point, Brett?"

"The point? She's avoiding me…thinks she'll be tarred with the same brush. After all, it's a time-honored plot, isn't it…wife and lover kill inconvenient husband?" He paused to look earnestly into Carol's eyes. "I didn't kill Mitchell. I don't know anything about it. I want you to make sure the cops understand that."

"Perhaps Christine is avoiding you because she thinks you did kill him," Carol said thoughtfully.

She got an immediate reaction. His voice was bitter as he said, "She knows I didn't, but she's safe, don't you think? Got an alibi, hasn't she? They haven't found that woman who could prove I was in Parramatta…I doubt if they've tried very hard. It's going to be so easy to pin it on me, isn't it!"

"It's a long way from that, Brett."

"Bourke wants to see me and Chris at the house this

86

morning. I'll have to leave soon."

"Together?"

"Yes. Why would he do that?"

Carol knew that Mark would want to see them interacting so he could probe for weaknesses that could be exploited later. It was also useful to confront suspects with the scene of the murder to see who would be most likely to crack under pressure. She said, "Perhaps it's convenient to see both of you at the same time."

Brett was pacing up and down, his lanky body awkward in the constricted space. Bourke had sent her a copy of the love letter found in Mitchell's desk with a note that it was definitely Brett's handwriting. She wondered if he realized such incriminating evidence was in police hands.

Carol said, "Are you and Christine lovers?"

"No!"

"Did Mitchell think you were?"

"Why should he? She's my sister-in-law and a friend. Nothing more."

Carol could remember the wording of the short letter Brett had written:

Chris my darling,
I can't tell you how much I hate to imagine you in someone else's arms. Letting someone else invade your sweet body. You know I love you and will do anything, anything for you. I remember that kiss and I burn. Please, dearest, think of me.

Brett

Carol became aware that Brett was watching her intently, his long frame bent like a spring about to rebound. He said, "Carol, you've got to find out who it is."

"I'd like to ask you about some of the people involved. For example, how do you get on with Fiona Brandstett?"

Brett narrowed his eyes. "That bitch?"

"I gather that means not well?"

He shrugged. "I hardly know her, although she'd say she was Chris's best friend." The sneer in his voice was unmistakable.

Carol said, "Tell me about her."

"There's nothing to tell. Fiona Brandstett and her permanently pissed husband fancy themselves something special. I don't know why Chris wastes her time on them."

Carol led him through a series of questions about the Brandstetts, but he stubbornly resisted anything but general comments, all unfavorable but lacking in detail. About Mitchell's business partners he was more expansive. In his opinion Gloria Tyne was an emotional time bomb ready to explode in someone's face. Mitchell had let drop a few comments that made him think his brother was scoring with Gloria, but if he was, he was being uncharacteristically careful. Mitchell had usually boasted to him about any conquests—not that there were many—but he hadn't said anything direct about Gloria Tyne.

Kurt Boardman? Couldn't stand the man—typical salesman, slippery and insincere. Didn't Carol agree? It appeared Kurt had been unwise enough to give Brett a few pointers on selling and Brett had not forgiven such impertinence. Privately, Carol considered Brett as needing all the selling tips he could get, but she nodded sympathetically as he denigrated his brother's partner.

"And of course Kurt blocked Mitchell's ideas of expansion every step of the way. Small man, small thinker—that's what Mitchell said, and I couldn't have put it better myself."

When Carol queried if Kurt Boardman could possibly be a murderer, Brett laughed contemptuously. "Him? The little bastard wouldn't have the guts!"

Asked about his brother's secretary, Rosie Lee, his manner changed. "Rosie? She's a darling…been with Mitchell for years and years…practically worshipped the ground he walked on…"

"Is it possible she was in love with him?"

Brett laughed aloud. "Rosie?" he said incredulously. "God! She's middle-aged!"

Carol resisted the comment that emotions didn't have a predetermined age limit, but she did allow an ironic note to creep into her voice as she said, "Perhaps I should have suggested a warm motherly love…"

Brett nodded. Rosie, although a childless widow, was certainly motherly. She had always been extremely nice to him and, in fact, had gone out of her way to help him get to Mitchell when Mitchell was playing hard to find.

The sullen resentment that seeped into his voice when he mentioned his brother was jarring. And, Carol reflected, something he should be intelligent enough to avoid now that he was a suspect for Mitchell's death.

"Brett, before I go, is there anything you haven't told me… even a small thing?"

There was a shadow of hesitation when he seemed to decide to speak or not to speak. Then he said, "No, nothing. I've told you everything. I just want you to put in a word for me, find out the way things are going, make sure…" He made an ineffectual gesture.

Carol's tone was dry. "That you're not charged with a murder you didn't commit."

Her words seemed almost to amuse him. Scooping the lock of hair from his eyes, he said, "We trust you Carol. Don't let us down."

Carol stopped at a public telephone and called up her answering machine. The first voice recorded was thick with belligerence. "Look, this is John Brandstett. Got that? I want to speak to you. It's urgent, so don't waste any time getting back to me." The second message was from Rosie Lee, wondering if Carol could possibly drop by today—nothing vital, but it could be important. The third made Carol's heart turn: Christine said, "Carol? Please, I'd like to see you."

John Brandstett hadn't bothered to leave a telephone number, but Carol presumed he would be at his office. She was put on hold for an irritating length of time and then Brandstett's brusque voice boomed in her ear. "Carol Ashton is it?"

Carol admitted that it was. Brandstett said curtly, "You saw my wife the other day. I wouldn't take too seriously anything she might have said. She's upset, of course."

"Is there any particular thing I should ignore?"

Brandstett, who sounded as if he had been drinking, seemed unaware of the sarcasm in her voice. He said, "What did you two talk about?"

"Surely Mrs. Brandstett can discuss the subjects with you."

There was a pause, then Brandstett said, "I'd be careful, if I were you. You're not on this case officially and you wouldn't like the publicity about Christine Tait and yourself, would you?"

She disregarded the jolt his words gave her, saying, "You are referring to...?"

He gave a bark of coarse laughter. "What's called in polite society unnatural practices. Want me to spell it out?"

"I wish you would," said Carol, "since I have no idea what it could be that I discussed with your wife that has led you to threaten me."

"Now look—"

Carol took pleasure in interrupting. "No, *you* look. You're making a clumsy effort to blackmail me. So clumsy that I can't work out what you want—"

It was Brandstett's turn to interrupt. "I didn't mention blackmail!"

Carol continued inexorably, "And your threat, I gather, is that you will accuse Christine Tait and myself of having a lesbian relationship. Is that correct?" She didn't wait for his reply, continuing, "Do you realize the implications of what you're doing?"

Into the silence that followed her words, Carol said sweetly, "I can't imagine for one moment that Christine Tait is going to be pleased to learn of your intentions."

Brandstett's voice was far less boorish as he said, "Christine doesn't have to know about this." It was obvious he was having second thoughts.

Carol pressed the advantage, saying with just a hint that she might be reasonable about the situation, "Mr. Brandstett, I don't take kindly to threats."

"You must have mistaken what I meant."

"Indeed? What did you mean?"

"I just don't want my wife involved in anything unpleasant. Christine is her friend, of course, and she'll stick by her, but to have these interviews, these constant intrusions into her privacy…"

She kept him talking, sourly amused at the moderation that was now in his voice. Like most bullies, he collapsed when his intended victim turned and showed unexpected fortitude. She was puzzled as to the real motive behind his clumsy attempt to intimidate her. Perhaps she had touched a nerve when speaking to Fiona yesterday. Brandstett finally rang off with a comment about his 'lapse of judgment' that put a wry smile on Carol's face.

Her smile disappeared when she replaced the receiver. Was this intimations of what was to come? Threats of exposure? Of having her private life laid out for public comment?

In contrast to Brandstett's rough voice, Rosie Lee cooed

into the phone, apologizing for worrying her at all. It was just that she did have some little bit of information that might help. Would Carol be interested in dropping by?

After that call, Carol hesitated, the receiver in her hand. She wanted to speak to Christine—she wanted to see her—but not till later. Not till Mark Bourke had put Brett and Christine together and shaken them to see what might happen.

TTB Computing's offices were as bright, efficient and impressive as they had been the week before. If Mitchell's death had cast a pall over the company it was not obvious to the casual eye. People peered into computer screens at work-stations, others frowned over sheets of printout or discussed esoteric matters in loud, confident voices.

Waiting at the reception desk, Carol could see Gloria Tyne in earnest conversation with a small group by one computer terminal and Kurt Boardman leading a similar gathering at another. From the corner Rosie Lee, on the telephone, waved across the open office, beckoning Carol to join her.

"Hectic," commented Carol with a nod towards the activity.

Rosie agreed. Gloria and Kurt had decided that Mitchell would have wanted the company to go on to greater successes and they were implementing their new development and sales phases immediately. Settling Carol in Mitchell's office, Rosie dispatched a junior employee for coffee and closed the door on the maelstrom.

Carol asked, "Does it upset you to see everything changing so soon after Mitchell's death?"

"It does, in a way…The funeral hasn't even been held yet."

Carol considered her closely. Motherly might be a word to apply to Rosie Lee, although there was a style to her clothing and an edge to her manner that suggested something less compliant in her nature. The tears that had continually filled her eyes on Friday morning had gone, but her face still showed the lines of grief and strain.

The coffee arrived. Carol leaned back, apparently relaxed, and Rosie played absently with a paper knife. At last she said, "Inspector, I know Gloria has denied ever threatening Mitchell. Detective Bourke advised me Gloria had said I was mistaken, or lying for some reason. I want you to know I was telling the absolute truth. Gloria *did* say she'd kill him."

"Since there were no other witnesses, it comes down to Gloria Tyne's word against yours."

Rosie nodded. "I accept that. What I can't accept is that she's lying about other things."

"Such as?"

"About Christine. Gloria has been saying, quite openly, that she's sure Christine and Brett killed Mitchell."

"Does she say she has any proof?"

"When I told her it was wrong to spread lies like that, Gloria said there was a letter from Brett to Christine—a letter that shows they were having an affair."

Carol didn't show her interest, merely remarking, "It's easy to make accusations…"

Rosie leaned forward earnestly. "Yes, it is…but Gloria claims she has a copy, and I believe her."

When Carol came out of the office, Gloria Tyne had disappeared, having left for a technical symposium in the city. Carol asked if she might use a phone, and squashed herself into a little area crowded with a computer console and stacks of perforated paper. She left a message for Mark Bourke detailing the claim that Gloria Tyne had made to Rosie Lee and then, after some hesitation, dialed the old familiar number.

Christine answered after a couple of rings. "Carol? I can't talk now, your Detective Bourke has just arrived—but tonight, please, can I see you tonight?"

Chapter 7

In the afternoon Carol went for a swim at Manly Beach where she tried to overcome the restless energy that filled her by battling the big waves rolling in from the Pacific. Then, finding herself too impatient to lie inert in the sun, she walked along the promenade eating a melting ice cream, dodging groups of arrogant seagulls, camera-toting tourists, and kids with zinc cream on their noses who should have been in school.

All the time she was thinking of Mitchell's death, trying out scenarios, guessing at motives, imagining how she would have accomplished it had she been his murderer.

To stab someone as large and powerful as Mitchell would take fortitude and determination…And why a knife, anyway? Such a weapon was not only difficult to conceal and likely to draw comment if noticed, but also it would have offered an unmistakable threat to Mitchell when brandished in the elegant room where he died. Why hadn't he disarmed his attacker, or at least tried to fend off the blow?

And there were motives to consider. Did the premeditated attack with a knife imply a particularly savage hatred...or was it the most convenient or familiar weapon at hand?

Pity none of the suspects happens to be a butcher, thought Carol wryly. Or, at the very least, a surgeon.

From her years in police work she knew well that the search for motives sometimes turned up surprising reasons for violence. Something that to an outsider was trivial could assume enormous importance to a potential murderer. In some cases it was a cumulative process—irritation after irritation, injustice after injustice—until finally there was enough mass to spontaneously ignite into white-hot hatred and violent action.

Christine? What strong enough motive could she have to risk killing Mitchell? With acid amusement Carol speculated why three years earlier Christine hadn't been willing to leave her husband for Carol's sake, but now might be capable of the far more drastic step of planning his murder to be with Brett. Christine obviously enjoyed her life as a member of the social set. Why disturb the universe by murdering Mitchell?

Perhaps unfairly, Carol had little difficulty visualizing Brett dispatching Mitchell to the afterlife. She had paid little attention to Brett when she had known him earlier—he had just been the younger, less charismatic brother—but now she found herself almost detesting him.

She had a reluctant thought: Is it Brett I dislike, or the fact that he and Christine may be lovers?

Her mind circled around the Brandstetts. They puzzled and intrigued her. John Brandstett she considered a blustering coward. His clumsy attempt to threaten her had been easy to puncture with a sharp word or two, but even so, cornered and desperate, couldn't he be dangerous? He was the type to drink his courage from a bottle and then act with stupid impetuosity…But this murder wasn't the fruit of a sudden impulse, it had been carefully planned…hadn't it?

Fiona Brandstett, however, was worthy of serious consideration. She had the steel in her personality that might make her capable of removing a threat permanently. But why Mitchell? What possible reason could she have to murder him when she had all the power to kill him socially? Mark Bourke's idea that Fiona might act to protect herself financially had some merit, but was it enough to drive her to the extreme hazards of homicide?

Then there were the three who worked with Mitchell: Rosie Lee, Gloria Tyne and Kurt Boardman. About Rosie Lee there was something ambivalent, something that didn't ring true. In contrast, Kurt Boardman had a kind of glib sincerity about him, but fairly or unfairly, wasn't that exactly what one would expect from a person whose career was sales?

Gloria Tyne was shaping up as the perfect suspect—emotionally intense, apparently deeply involved with Mitchell. And reported as threatening his life the day before. What more could one ask? In most murder cases, the most obvious suspect was the person who had committed the crime. Even so, Mark was a long way from arresting her…Motive, opportunity and an erratic personality were not enough to build a watertight case.

The telephone was ringing when she opened the door. Tripping over Sinker and Jeffrey who were determined to overcome the indignity of being put outside, she snatched up the receiver. It was Bourke.

"Carol? We've got it! The knife!"

He was as pleased as if he had discovered it himself. Two children playing in a quiet leafy suburban street a few minutes' drive from the Taits' house had lost a ball down the opening to a storm water drain. The steel grating in the gutter had been loose, so they had finally pried it up and clambered down under the overhang of the curb to look for their lost ball. What they had found had been far more exciting. Lying shining on a bed of leaves was a broad-bladed knife.

"Thank God for people who don't mind their own business," said Bourke, going on to explain how a neighbor had seen them playing with the knife and had called police when she realized the possible significance of what they had found.

The knife, an expensive imported culinary implement from Germany, had been washed, but there were still traces of human blood and Bourke was sure it would be AB Negative, Mitchell's blood type. There were no fingerprints, except for those of the children who had found it.

"There's a faint chance we'll pick up something from point of sale," said Bourke. "Who knows what might have been charged to an account?"

"Would this particular murderer be that careless?"

Carol could picture the shrug that accompanied Bourke's words as he said, "We could be lucky. People can be caught out over the simplest things."

She was impatient to know what had happened with Christine and Brett. "I gather you didn't arrest anyone this morning?"

"Not through lack of trying, Carol. I was poised to jot down a confession from a weeping Christine, but she remained obstinately dry-eyed throughout."

Bourke had walked Brett and Christine through every detail of their arrival at the house and discovery of the body. They both stuck religiously to their original statements. They had driven into the driveway almost simultaneously at about two-fifteen, parking their cars at the front of the house. Christine hadn't put her car in the double garage as she intended to go out again, so she didn't see Mitchell's car and therefore had no idea he was home. Everything seemed quite normal—the front door was locked, as usual, and neither noticed anything wrong as they walked into the hall.

They went into the kitchen, Christine started making coffee and then remembered that a painting Brett had particularly admired had just come back from cleaning and reframing. They went to the lounge room to view it, discovering Mitchell's body. It was apparent he was quite dead so they made no attempt to revive him. Brett, by his own description, was overcome with grief, sitting stunned and weeping while Christine had the presence of mind to call the police and her own doctor.

"Any inconsistencies?" asked Carol.

"Not a one. Everything fits smoothly, there's no unaccounted time and no unusual behavior—if anything, it's too pat."

"*Was* there a cleaned, reframing painting?"

"Indeed there was, Carol. How unkind to doubt I would ask to see it."

"And Brett's love letter?"

Bourke sighed. "Ah, the letter. Bit of an anticlimax, I'm afraid, since I was hoping for some drama and beating of breasts. Both of them took it quite calmly. Either I played it the wrong way, or they already knew I was about to whip it out and confront them with it. Brett Tait freely admitted being the writer, but said he'd written it when drunk and never thought Christine would take it seriously."

"And Christine?"

"She put on what I can only describe as an appropriate expression for such trying times."

Carol was growing impatient. "Come on, Mark!"

"Basically, she was convincing. Said the letter had

embarrassed her, she thought Brett had got a bit carried away, and that the best course of action was to pretend she'd never received it. Said she put it away and forgot about it."

"Where?"

"She had her own desk. Said it was in with her letters, so if someone was looking for it there was no problem finding it."

Carol had a high opinion of Bourke's instincts. She said, "What impressions do you have?"

"She was all right, sort of relaxed but regretful, if I can put it that way. *He* explained a little too much."

Carol knew exactly what Bourke meant. It was the person anxious to cover every possible contingency who generated suspicion, if for no other reason than this indicated detailed preparation in order to cover every angle.

Bourke said, "Brett was keen to account for that immortal line *I remember that kiss and I burn*. He said it was a drunken kiss he gave Christine at her birthday party—a kiss, he was sure, she wouldn't even remember. Obligingly, Christine said everyone had kissed her on her birthday and no, she didn't remember Brett's efforts in particular."

"Did you get the impression they'd rehearsed any of this?"

"It's hard to say. Brett Tait looked nervous. Christine looked self-possessed—very self-possessed."

Irritated by the tone in his voice, Carol thought, That doesn't make her guilty! Then she chided herself for her emotional reaction. She might feel deeply that Chris was completely innocent, but proving it beyond doubt was another thing altogether.

Bourke broke into her thoughts, asking her about her conversation with Rosie Lee that morning. After Carol had detailed Rosie's accusations about Gloria Tyne, Bourke said, "You'll love this next bit of information, Carol. It seems that the day before he died Mitchell fired our Rosie."

"Fired her! No one's given any hint of trouble between

her and Mitchell. And she's played grief-stricken secretary to the hilt."

"Well, according to the company accountant, Mitchell gave firm instructions to give Rosie the heave-ho about a week ago. There was to be a termination sweetener of six months full salary and the whole thing was to be kept quiet."

"Any concrete reason?"

"Mitchell didn't elaborate and when I fronted her Rosie's account is rather different—she says she wasn't pushed, she jumped. Seems Rosie decided to resign some time ago and had finally persuaded a reluctant Mitchell to accept it. There was, she says, no animosity, no problem—just that work was taking up too much of her time and she thought she'd move somewhere where she could have shorter hours."

Carol was doing a rapid reappraisal of Rosie's role in the drama. To be fired after so many years of a close working relationship with Mitchell might well cause the most bitter resentment. "Did she say why she didn't mention it after the murder?"

Bourke's tone was mocking. "Because, she says, it no longer applied. She could see TTB Computing was in chaos, what with Mitchell's death and all, so she's staying on to help."

Bourke went on to say that he didn't believe Rosie's story of resigning. He thought Mitchell Tait had become tired of her interference over his relationship with Gloria Tyne. "You know," he said, "I think the whole Gloria Tyne thing is one of this case's most notable red herrings. My money's still on Christine."

Carol's voice had a bite in it. "She has an alibi."

"Ah, Carol," said Bourke, "she only has an alibi for as long as Fiona Brandstett is willing to give her one. And for all we know, Fiona and Christine are in it together."

"Do you have any evidence to support this theory?" said Carol, not bothering to keep the skepticism from her voice.

"You've always encouraged me," said Bourke flippantly, "to use my creative imagination—and that's what I'm doing." A pause, then he said more seriously, "Carol, there's something I want to say."

"Then say it," she said shortly.

"I've never intruded in any way into your personal life—"

"No, you haven't."

Her tone was a warning he disregarded. "But you're running such a risk...what I mean is, if either Christine Tait or Brett Tait go to trial, I can't see how you can avoid being involved at a personal level. Do you understand what I mean?"

"Of course I do," she snapped. "You think my affair with Christine will be brought up in court."

She heard him sigh. "If you get out now, take your trip overseas, maybe—"

"No."

His voice was subdued. "I'm sorry I said anything."

Her anger evaporated. "Mark, you're a good friend, but I don't want to discuss this. Okay?"

"Okay," he said, resignation in his tone.

Carol moved her shoulders to ease the tension she felt. Christine dressed in jeans and sneakers was as alluring as Christine in an expensive dress or Christine in—her mind shied away—nothing at all.

Christine smiled at her across the kitchen. "Do you remember that first kiss? It was here, by the sink."

"I remember."

Here in the house where Mitchell had died, Carol felt awkward and uncomfortable. She kept her tone even, saying, "That letter from Brett —"

"You've seen it?"

"Yes. It gives him a motive…and you, too, perhaps."

Christine shook her head. "You don't believe that. I had no reason to kill Mitchell."

"John Brandstett tried a little gentle blackmail on me today. Why would that be?"

Christine moved towards her, eyes intent. "I've no idea," she said absently. She stopped in front of Carol, almost touching her.

Carol was aware that her breath was singing in her throat. She said, "Chris…"

Christine's eyes were on Carol's mouth. She said, "When we kissed, Carol, that first time, I felt as though I had never kissed anyone before."

A sense of inevitability—the conviction that the day had a sharp purpose—had been with Carol since morning. She stood still as Christine took that last step. Thigh to thigh, breast to breast, fire in Christine's mouth.

Carol kept her lips resolutely closed, back stiff against temptation. Christine ran her tongue along Carol's tight mouth, tongue pressing, flickering, demanding entry.

With a groan Carol opened her lips and was immediately afire. Christine had her arms about her, hands pressing against her buttocks, heat to heat.

"Love me," she whispered into Carol's mouth.

Carol put her hands against her shoulders and pushed her away. "Love you?" she said. Bitter anger made her voice brittle. "I loved you once…and where did it get me?"

"Dearheart."

She turned away. "No."

Christine's voice was soft. "Are you running away from me?"

"Very possibly," said Carol with cold amusement.

Sybil had been persuaded by teacher friends to go to a school reunion dinner and was late coming home, so Carol was alone with her thoughts. She showered and got into bed, hoping to blot out the day with sleep. The moment she closed her eyes images of Christine sprang into eager life. She forced herself to lie with her hands behind her head gazing at the ceiling. She wanted to be rational, to assess with detachment any new details about the case. But it was impossible. Against her will her body tensed with an involuntary tremor as she remembered Christine's mouth and the husky promise of her voice. She was both ashamed and excited by the pictures in her imagination—ashamed that the anger and resentment she felt against Christine could be so easily defeated by the demands of passion, excited by the surge of heat that ran from her thighs and into her belly at the thought of Christine's touch.

And Sybil—wasn't she being unfaithful to Sybil? They had never really promised each other anything, but wasn't there an unspoken agreement based on a growing love between them?

Love. Carol turned the word over in her mind. Whom did she love? Christine, whose rejection had once almost destroyed her and who could still ignite her body with effortless power? Or Sybil, whose veneer of passive detachment hid depths of passionate feeling?

How would she feel if she were Sybil? Betrayed? Angry? Jealous?

Jealousy, the darker side of love—was that the force that had driven a knife up into Mitchell's chest?

Chapter 8

Tuesday couldn't decide whether to be wet or dry. The sun shone fitfully, bright and hard, and then clouds clumped, darkened, spat inconsequential rain, only to be blown away and again replaced with shattering brightness.

Bourke had suggested that he pick her up so that they could discuss developments in the case. He was, as always, right on time.

"The things," he said, leaning across to open the passenger door for her, "that people just neglect to tell you."

"Such as?" Carol inquired.

"Such as the interesting little fact that Kurt Boardman and Gloria Tyne were romantically inclined about a year ago, just after his divorce became final. Indeed, Carol, they were involved in what Trisha Moore, a secretary at TTB

Computing, describes as a really deep relationship."

Carol smiled at his ironic tone. She said, "Trisha Moore would know?"

Bourke exhibited mock shock. "How could you doubt it? Not only has she been elected social secretary two years running, she also has a lively interest in the affairs, and I use that word advisedly, of the staff as a whole."

"So the suggestion is that Mitchell Tait took over where Kurt Boardman left off."

Bourke shook his head. "Kurt didn't leave off—he was shouldered out of the way by Tait. Couple of nasty scenes between the two of them, according to Trisha."

"And Gloria had no say in this at all?"

"The word is that Gloria got a charge out of the whole situation. She played Kurt and Mitchell off against each other and then stood back and enjoyed the results."

Carol raised her eyebrows. "Rosie Lee didn't mention this and neither did anyone else. I wonder why."

Bourke said, "Come with me and we'll find out." He leered at her suggestively. "I'll show you a good time, lady!"

"Best offer I've had all day," said Carol with a grin, adding, "I'm not having a good one, you understand."

TTB Computing hummed with industry. Carol had the fanciful thought that as she and Bourke walked through the front door a button was pushed to start the cast on their appointed activities—clustering around screens, carrying sheets of printout or engaging in deep technical discussions.

Whenever they had been together on a case before, Carol had outranked Mark Bourke, so their working relationship had been ruled by her seniority. This investigation was Bourke's case, complicated by her unofficial status and the fact that she had a personal involvement. Mark was showing her his discomfort with the unusual situation by his occasional awkwardness. Usually relaxed and amusing, he seemed uncharacteristically tense, and Carol was constantly aware that she must be careful not to step into his territory without invitation.

"Trisha Moore," he said to Carol, "is going to be awfully impressed by you."

He appeared to be accurate in his assessment. Carol smiled at the bouncy young secretary with the heavy eye makeup who repeated Carol's name as though memorizing it for future reference.

"Detective Inspector Carol Ashton."

"Yes."

"I've seen you on television."

Although she had often heard this, Carol had never been sure how to respond to the comment, so she nodded, almost expecting to be asked for her autograph.

Prompted by Bourke, Trisha launched into an account of the dynamics of the relationships between Gloria, Kurt and Mitchell. From Bourke's expression Carol was sure Trisha was embroidering her original statement rather freely, but the essence of her story remained the same. Kurt and Gloria had been close but then Mitchell had taken over and left Kurt out in the cold.

Carol said, "Would everyone in the office have known about the relationship between Gloria Tyne and Kurt Boardman?"

Trisha thought so—"why hide it? Anyway, Kurt had been that keen…"

"Very much in love with her?"

Trisha enthusiastically agreed. "Absolutely! Broke Kurt's heart when she dropped him. You could tell."

Carol observed that it was a very friendly office. Trisha had to agree with that. "Absolutely! Everyone's on first-name terms, even Mitch."

Carol, remembering how he would grimace when someone had the temerity to shorten his name, said, "You mean Mitchell Tait?"

She did. Trisha also noted that Rosie Lee had asked her not to gossip about Kurt and Gloria because (mimicking Rosie's precise intonation with startling accuracy) "It lowers the tone of the office to discuss personal matters."

"Was there anything in particular you weren't to mention?"

Although not absolutely sure, Trisha had an idea it was when Kurt got so upset, accused Mitchell of swindling him and then threatened him.

Carol avoided looking at Mark Bourke, saying offhandedly, "Oh? Could you give some details?"

Trisha was pleased to comply. As Carol and Bourke walked to Kurt Boardman's office, Bourke said, "Interesting, eh?"

"Absolutely," said Carol with a grin.

Kurt was waiting for them. Sober and subdued, he shook hands then ushered them to seats. He said with a trace of tired amusement, "I know why you're here. Trisha told me what she'd said after she first spoke to Detective Bourke. Frankly, it surprises me she was the only person to mention my relationship with Gloria."

Carol sat back silently and let Bourke radiate sympathetic inquiry. "Was it widely known?"

Smoothing his hair across his balding head, Kurt said, "I suppose some people found it amusing—Gloria going with me—but it probably didn't strike them as important enough to remember. After all, it was a year ago."

"You didn't mention it when I first interviewed you."

Kurt looked at Bourke with an ironic twist to his mouth.

"Surely you didn't expect me to hand you a motive on a plate, even if it was a weak one?"

"Weak?"

Kurt began to play absently with the shiny executive toy on his desk. "I won't pretend it wasn't serious at the time—for me, that is. I can't speak for Gloria." He cleared his throat. "But it was a year ago and I got over it relatively quickly."

"You're in another relationship now?" said Bourke.

"No—nothing long-term, anyway. My divorce was upsetting...and then Gloria..."

Bourke flipped open his notebook and consulted a page. Carol smiled a little to herself. It was a useful way to gently intimidate by suggesting the existence of certain, but as yet unmentioned, evidence.

Unable to bear the silence, Kurt said, "You've heard I threatened Mitchell. It's true—I did. But it was in the heat of the moment and in a few days it was all forgotten."

"What did you say to him?"

Kurt looked embarrassed. "Oh, something juvenile, like I'll kill you for this. Never really meant a word of it."

"Do you recall mentioning something about Mitchell swindling you?"

"I'd lost my temper. I said anything that came into my mind."

"*Did* you believe he'd been swindling you in some way?"

"At the time I might have. I don't remember." Kurt paused, straightened his tie, said, "Look, I made a complete fool of myself. The walls of Mitchell's office are hardly soundproof and I was very loud. It makes me cringe to remember it, actually."

Another pause, then Kurt's sales persona began to reassert itself. The unpleasant subject dealt with, he began to loosen up, become expansive, grow warmer. Carol watched the transformation with fascination. At one moment he had been a middle-aged, stout, balding, unsuccessful lover—now he was visibly becoming the confident, charming and outgoing personality she had met before.

Bourke looked at her with surprise when, after a few relaxed comments from Kurt, Carol asked, "Do you know Fiona Brandstett well?"

"I know her husband better—John Brandstett's company was underwriting the share float. Gloria's the one who gets on with Fiona."

Carol blinked at this. Fiona and Gloria seemed to her diametrically opposed in every possible way. She was about to pursue the matter when Gloria flung open the office door, her hair as wild as the look she gave Kurt. "What are you saying about me?" she demanded.

"About you?" he replied in astonishment. "Nothing."

Rosebud mouth tight with anger, she turned to Bourke and Carol. "It's no use raking up this thing with Kurt—it didn't mean anything at the time and it certainly doesn't mean anything now."

Bourke said, "Could we see the letter you have? The one Brett Tait wrote."

Gloria's dark eyes narrowed. "I don't know what you're talking about."

Bourke was patient. "We've been told you have a letter written to Mrs. Tait. Is that true?"

The anger was rapidly fading from Gloria's face, replaced by a watchful intensity. Kurt had sunk back in his chair and was watching her fixedly. Today Gloria was wearing a faintly grubby gypsy blouse, full black skirt and large gold hoop earrings. Carol suddenly had an insight into why both Kurt and Mitchell might find her so attractive—there was a kind of dark integrity to her personality and a hint of compelling sensuality about her movements.

"I haven't got the letter. Mitchell just showed it to me."

110

Bourke was brisk. "When?"

Gloria tossed her head impatiently. "I don't know! A week ago—ten days. Does it matter?"

"Yes, it does matter."

Frowning, she considered. "Okay, it was last week...last Wednesday, actually. His wife was up at their holiday place at Pearl Beach, so we had some time together."

Bourke was politely insistent. "Now that you remember when you saw it, can you remember the contents?"

Gloria's shrug was elaborate. "Not really—something about how Brett would do anything for Christine. And perhaps he did."

"Meaning?"

"Oh, come on!" she said with irritation. "Don't bother playing dumb with me. If Christine Tait's got an alibi, then obviously she got Brett to do her dirty work."

Kurt said warningly, "Gloria..."

She looked at him with a kind of rough affection. "Look, Kurt, you can't spend your life shutting your eyes to what really goes on in the world. That's always been your problem—you just can't face anything that's going to upset you, can you?"

Carol glimpsed an unsuspected facet in Gloria Tyne's personality. Perhaps she and Bourke had underestimated her, had been too swift to put her in a category marked "moody and intense." A look had passed between Kurt and Gloria. Carol felt like an intruder upon something private and surprisingly sweet. From Kurt it was a warning springing from the warmth of love; Gloria returned an almost imperceptible smile of acceptance and contrition.

Gloria turned back to Bourke, saying calmly, "Mitchell's death has upset me very much. Perhaps I haven't been altogether rational. It seemed to me Christine had to be involved. As for Brett—it seems insane to think he'd kill his own brother—but someone did. And I saw the letter."

Bourke questioned patiently and thoroughly, but elicited very little else. Gloria had no idea how Mitchell had obtained the letter—he had ignored her questions. And who said she had a copy of it? She never claimed she did.

Bourke's eyes went to Carol. She nodded, excused herself, and went to find Rosie Lee.

En route Carol literally ran into Trisha Moore, who was obviously lurking near Kurt's office with the intent to see and hear as much as possible. She blushed a little at Carol's knowing smile, saying defensively, "Thought I'd check to see if anyone wanted tea or coffee or anything…"

"I wonder if you could help me," said Carol.

"Absolutely!"

Carol drew her aside to a vacant work station and began to ask her a series of gently phrased but probing questions. Trisha's lively interest in all things personal and private was an asset in an investigation such as this. Carol asked her opinion on personalities, her recollections of the day Mitchell died, and finally, "Is there anything else at all you could tell me, that might be of help?"

Trisha pondered.

Carol knew Trisha might obligingly create something meaningful from her active imagination, but it was a risk worth taking. A chance remark, some apparently insignificant detail—these could be devastating when combined with other information.

Trisha was shaking her head with regret. "Can't think of anything." She frowned, then said, "When Mitch was leaving the office that morning, Rosie followed him out, talking all the way."

"Did you hear what she was saying?"

"Something about reconsidering. She sounded a bit upset, but he was brushing her off, you know, sort of didn't have time to listen."

Carol thought it likely that Rosie was asking Mitchell not to terminate her employment. She said, "Was she still upset when she came back?"

"She didn't come back."

Carol remembered Rosie Lee commenting that the Wednesday Mitchell died she had had so much work to do she didn't even take a break for lunch, but ate a sandwich at her desk.

"How do you know that?"

Trisha assumed an expression of one who has been unfairly exploited. "I had to answer all the telephone calls she usually takes for Mitch. It was a bit much, because Kurt and Gloria were out too, so I spent most of the morning taking messages."

"She did return?"

"Oh, yes. I'm not sure exactly when, though. It was lunchtime...somewhere around one-thirty, I think."

Carol didn't let the interest she felt show on her face. It was conceivable that Rosie Lee had followed Mitchell home to plead for her job, argued with him, killed him and then hurried back to the office.

Without hope of being obeyed she asked Trisha to keep their discussion confidential and then went in search of Rosie Lee.

Carol selected a tone of friendly interest as she said to Rosie Lee, "You did say yesterday that Gloria Tyne claimed to have a copy of a letter from Brett Tait to his brother's wife."

"I suppose she's denying it. Typical!"

Rosie seemed to be unraveling. Her hair was not quite as smoothly combed, her face seemed older, her fingers played incessantly with a metal paper knife. Carol had a momentary vision of Rosie's hand holding another knife—the one used to

113

dispatch Mitchell six days ago.

Carol was now convinced Rosie would say anything to put Gloria in a bad light. She said, "Gloria claims she never mentioned having a copy."

Rosie seemed to deflate. She looked away. "I may have been mistaken about that…" She straightened. "Gloria *did* say she'd seen an incriminating letter. She's not denying that too?"

Carol smiled pleasantly. "No, not at all. There is one other thing. Did you ask anyone not to mention the fact that Kurt Boardman had threatened Mitchell?"

Rosie nodded with tired certainty. "That would be Trisha Moore telling you that. Well, it's quite true. Trisha's good-hearted, but she's young and thoughtless. Inclined to gossip and hurt other people's feelings without ever meaning to. Last year, when Kurt and Gloria were breaking up, Kurt said some stupid things to Mitchell—things he didn't mean. Unfortunately Trisha heard most of it, so I asked her not to repeat anything."

"It didn't occur to you that this information might be relevant now?"

"That Kurt threatened Mitchell? Of course not. It wasn't serious and Kurt would never hurt anyone."

It seemed to Carol this must be the thousandth time she had heard such a statement—and many times it was made about a person later charged with murder. She said with asperity, "Someone *did* hurt Mitchell Tait."

Rosie shook her head. "Not Kurt. He couldn't."

"Even for Gloria Tyne?" said Carol, deliberately needling.

"Even for her," replied Rosie, not bothering to hide her contempt.

Carol said, "One last thing…"

Shoulders tensing, Rosie waited. Carol said, "I thought I understood you to say you didn't leave the office the day Mitchell died…"

She waited. In the silence she heard Rosie sigh. "All right, Inspector, I admit I wasn't here the entire time. I know you're going to ask me why I lied, but it's more that I neglected to tell you…"

"Some would call that lying by omission."

"Please try to understand…" Rosie dabbed at tears. Carol kept a neutral expression, wondering how much of this might be an act to gain a sympathetic hearing.

Her silence forced Rosie to continue. "When Mitchell died that horrible way…I didn't want to get involved…I hadn't done anything wrong…"

"Why did you walk out of the office with him at ten-fifteen and not come back until much later?"

Rosie leaned back in her chair and looked at Carol defiantly. "Do you really want to know? I was fed up—tired of being taken for granted—I told Mitchell how I felt and then I stalked off, sulking you might say, and spent a couple of hours just shopping, wasting time, that sort of thing. After a while I thought what a fool I was, so I came back to work."

"Do you know what time you returned?"

"Not really. About one, I think."

"Not later?"

Rosie looked at her sharply. "Later? Maybe, but only a few minutes."

Carol asked her next question casually. "Were you fed up, as you say, because Mitchell had fired you?"

Rosie stood, indignation, real or assumed, on her face. "That isn't true. I've already explained to Detective Sergeant Bourke that I resigned. I can't even begin to imagine why anyone would say otherwise."

"Mitchell said otherwise."

Rosie was decisive. "He's dead, so he can't defend himself. Whoever told you that is lying. A lot of people are lying to you, Inspector."

Carol and Bourke sat in his car and compared notes.

"Mark, I think we've undersold Gloria."

He nodded. "I'm inclined to agree. And I think the view I've taken of the relationship between Gloria and Kurt Boardman has been too simplistic. He's not just a rejected lover scorned—and she's certainly got more to her than meets the eye." He grinned at her. "How about you take on Gloria in one of your feminist woman-to-woman talks while I do a macho man-to-man with Kurt?"

He laughed aloud at her expression. "Carol," he said, "I can't tell if you're reacting to the feminist or the macho—or is it both?"

After Bourke had dropped her back home, Carol, acting on an impulse, looked up the address and then drove to Brett Tait's office. It was upstairs in a tired suburban shopping center, one cramped room in a row of little shabby business offices, all of which looked to be lurching towards bankruptcy.

She made her way down a hallway of various shades of grubby brown until she found Tait Enterprises. Brett raised his eyes, then stood up in consternation as he recognized her. "Carol, what are you doing here?"

She realized his reaction was embarrassment at being found in such surroundings. The office was crowded with rolls of upholstery material, boxes of brochures, a confusion of papers. The desk had coffee rings on its surface and an overflowing ashtray. Brett moved quickly to take some samples off a dusty chair, brush it off and indicate she should sit. All this was watched by a bored and pimply young girl whose hands rested slackly on the keys of a typewriter.

"Uh, Annie, go downstairs and get yourself a cup of coffee or something."

When Annie didn't move, he added, "Use petty cash." This suggestion led to some activity and, after delay for the collection of her handbag and petty cash, Annie left with a speculative sideways glance at Carol.

Brett pushed back the lock of hair from his forehead. "These are just temporary offices," he said. "Be moving soon into larger premises."

Carol wanted to keep him off balance. She said bluntly, "I've been talking to Mark Bourke. Things don't look good for you, Brett."

He rubbed his fingers across his mouth. "I suppose you mean the letter? They don't believe me, do they...that I never really meant it."

"Would you believe that story?"

His shoulders slumped in defeat. "Probably not. Carol, what's going to happen?"

"I imagine the idea will be to tie you as closely as possible to Christine to suggest you planned Mitchell's death together— or that you did it on your own, convinced you'd win Christine once she was free. Either way you're in trouble."

"Will you help me?"

"Yes, if you tell me the truth. Are you and Christine lovers?"

"Not exactly."

"What does that mean?"

"We made love once. That's all."

Carol was astonished at the raw anger that swept through her. If Christine had been there she would have slapped her. She kept her voice steady as she asked for details.

Brett kept his eyes on the surface of the tattered desk. "I love Chris. I've loved her for years, but I never said, or did, anything about it. Then on her birthday, last year, I kissed her…and she opened her mouth and kissed me back. I couldn't think straight—that's why I wrote that letter."

"And you meant every word."

"Yes."

"You lied about that."

"I wanted to protect Chris. If they know we're lovers…"

Carol smiled grimly. "If they know you're lovers they'll also know you've got a motive to get rid of Mitchell. Is that it?"

Brett nodded slowly.

Angered by his hangdog look, Carol said brutally, "When did you have intercourse with her?"

He winced at the word. "Two months ago, when Mitchell was on a business trip." He looked at her earnestly. "That's the only time—honestly, Carol."

"You were both overcome with guilt?"

Brett straightened at her sarcasm. "It's odd you should take that attitude, Carol. You had a long-standing affair with her yourself."

Carol looked away. "You're absolutely right, Brett."

There was a sticky silence, echoing with the words both of them could say, but wouldn't. Brett broke it with an explanation. "Look, Chris was the one who said it was impossible, that we should stop it before it really began. I was—I am—in love with her. I wanted it to go on. Mitchell might have been my brother, but Chris means more to me than anyone ever has before."

"Enough to kill for her?"

"No. Not that much." He leaned forward and put his hand on her arm. "Carol, please believe me. I really didn't kill him and I don't know who did."

"I want you to go through the day Mitchell died again. Don't groan at me, Brett. There might be something you've forgotten that will tie in with something else."

Brett repeated the details of his visits to prospective customers, his lunchtime at the Parramatta McDonald's with the still unlocated sales representative, and then his subsequent aimless wanderings until he met Christine.

"She rang me early Wednesday morning to remind me about meeting her, but I hadn't forgotten…I'd been looking forward to it, being alone with her."

"You were going to discuss persuading Mitchell to put more money into your business?"

"Yes—and I also wanted to talk to Chris about how I felt. I didn't hurry. You know as well as I do how often Chris is late." He hesitated, then added, "But she was on time."

"You didn't actually turn into the drive one after the other?"

He frowned. "Chris was just turning off the engine. We said hello, then Chris opened the front door and we went in."

Carol was intent. "Brett, I want you to use your imagination to recreate that moment when you entered the house. Did you see, hear, smell anything?"

Brett wrinkled his forehead in concentration. "Chris had a key, she opened the door, went in first. She was saying something about how hot houses get when they're closed up all day. We walked down the hall, she turned on the air-conditioning, we went into the kitchen. It was quiet, that sort of hush you get on hot afternoons." He shook his head. "Nothing was unusual. The kitchen was tidy, everything in its place. And then we went into the front room and found Mitchell."

"Who found him? You? Christine?"

"I don't know who saw him first—Chris, I think. I remember thinking it was all play-acting, that Mitchell would laugh and get up and say 'I fooled you, didn't I?' But he couldn't get up because he was dead."

She took him through the next half hour, asking for details

on what was said and what was done. "Chris was so much better than me. She took over. I was a write-off."

Carol looked sympathetic, but she was considering that perhaps the shock and grief that had paralyzed Brett at that point was actually caused by the extreme emotional stress of viewing the body of the brother he had slaughtered an hour and a half earlier.

Annie returned, still looking speculatively sideways. Carol smiled at her, and then at Brett. "Call me if you think of anything else," she said, reassuringly. "I'm sure this will all be settled soon."

One way or another, she thought.

Chapter 9

Wednesday was unpleasantly humid with a dull blanket of cloud sweating the land. Sybil woke with a headache and a weary discontent. She watched Carol come in from her early morning run silent and withdrawn, nibble at a piece of toast and then push the rest of her breakfast away. Sybil looked at Carol's beautiful hands, the black opal ring which she was now absently twisting on her finger, and said, "What's the matter?"

Carol looked up, green eyes blank. "Nothing."

"Can we spend some time together today?"

"I'm sorry, I'm caught up. How about we go out for dinner tonight?"

Sybil knew if she asked the question she would blight her day. Even so, she said, "It's Christine you're seeing, isn't it?"

"Yes."

Sybil felt indignant. "For God's sake, Carol—the whole day?"

"Christine rang me this morning from Pearl Beach. She's gone to stay at the holiday home there for a few days. I'm seeing Gloria Tyne first thing this morning, then I'll drive up. It's only an hour and a half by car."

Sybil couldn't prevent a note of ire in her voice as she said, "So you're spending the day alone together. Sure you'll be free tonight? No doubt she'll ask you to stay."

Carol sounded irritated. "Perhaps she will, but I have a date with you this evening."

Don't say too much, thought Sybil, and immediately ignored her own advice. She heard the anger flicker in her voice as she replied, "Are you enjoying this, Carol? Playing us off against each other? Does it please you to be the object of such attention from two would-be lovers?"

Sybil's heat made Carol's voice temperate. "I'll meet you at the restaurant…or do you want to forget it?"

"No, I don't want to forget it!" snapped Sybil. "I'll book Alfredo's at Balmoral Beach for eight. Okay?"

"Okay."

In the pause that followed, Sybil wondered bleakly why she was bothering to fight at all. Wasn't it easier to sit detached on the sidelines and wait to see if Carol went back to Christine or stayed with her?

Hell, Sybil thought with a wry inward smile, I'm getting awfully melodramatic!

She leaned over and kissed Carol full on the mouth. "Be there!" she said pseudo-threatening, "Or I breaka you face!"

Carol was not surprised to discover that Gloria Tyne lived in trendy inner-city Balmain. A suburb once filled with working class families, it had undergone a relentless gentrification that had driven out all but a few pockets of the original population. Now its terrace houses were filled with upwardly mobile professionals whose interests in preserving the ambience of the area did not include maintaining the previous social mix.

Balmain's streets, many of which had been designated one-way in an apparently random system, seemed planned to confuse. After missing the turn twice and consulting her street directory several times, Carol eventually drew up outside Gloria's address in the middle of a row of terrace houses, each one huddled tight against its neighbor in an architectural depiction of together we stand, divided we fall.

The high front gate was locked and Carol had to push the bell button several times before Gloria's disheveled head popped over the cast iron of the top veranda. "Oh, it's you," she said ungraciously, disappearing to reappear at the front gate moments later with even less enthusiasm on her face.

Although Carol reminded herself of the insight she had gained while watching Kurt and Gloria yesterday, she found it difficult to conceive that this untidy, frowning woman had a shaft of sweetness in her nature.

Gloria led the way down the narrow hall to a kitchen stacked with unwashed dishes and discarded food containers. "Coffee? Tea?" she asked with peremptory hospitality.

In spite of her doubts about the probable cleanliness of any cup or mug in these surroundings, Carol politely asked for black coffee with the thought that a menial task might relax Gloria's guard a little. It was an unrealized hope. Gloria continued to regard her with narrowed eyes as she flung a spoonful of instant coffee into a sketchily rinsed mug. She thumped it down in front of Carol. "We can sit here, in the kitchen. You won't be long, will you?"

Carol smiled at her.

At once Gloria seemed disconcerted. Then an answering

grin appeared. "I can be totally impossible, can't I?"

Carol's smile widened. "Sort of."

"After you and Detective Bourke had gone yesterday, Kurt read me the riot act."

Carol raised an inquiring eyebrow.

"Kurt thinks I'm giving you the wrong impression."

"What impression is that?"

"You'd make a good psychiatrist," said Gloria. "I can imagine you always sitting there calmly, no matter what horrific things people say to you."

"Have you got something horrific to say?"

Gloria was amused. "Hate to disappoint you—but no." Her smile faded. "Do you know who killed Mitchell?"

"Not yet."

After considering her soberly for a few moments, Gloria said, "I know you want to clear Christine. That's why you're here."

Carol spoke with conviction. "I don't believe Christine had anything to do with Mitchell's death, so that means someone else murdered him. That's all I'm doing—finding that someone else."

"And you'd like to try Kurt, or for that matter, me, for size?"

"I'm not trying to frame anybody, if that's what you mean. All I want is the truth."

Gloria leaned forward, and, as she spoke, Carol saw again the current of kindness under the brittle shell of her personality. "Kurt is a good person. I hurt him very much when I took up with Mitchell and he was angry with both of us, but after a while he accepted what had happened. He's not the type to bear a grudge for months and then do something about it. Maybe you're prejudiced against him because he's a salesman. God knows, *I* was before I knew him well."

"What's your relationship now?"

Gloria's voice was sincere as she presented her open palms in a gesture of honesty. "Kurt and I are friends—close, loving friends. Nothing more. Nothing less."

A thought skimmed across Carol's mind. Gloria was quite capable of studying body language and then deliberately mimicking the gestures and expressions of a totally straightforward and reliable person. She observed, "Kurt doesn't have a firm alibi."

Pursing her rosebud mouth, Gloria said, "Neither do I, really."

"So it would be possible for either of you—or both of you—to have murdered Mitchell?"

"Anything's possible, Inspector. In this case, however, I know I didn't. And I'm sure Kurt wouldn't. Violence just isn't in his nature."

"You know," said Carol reflectively, "very often, when someone is unmasked as a murderer, his or her nearest and dearest say something just like that. It's hard to accept that a person you know well—someone you're fond of—could kill."

"Thank you for sharing that with me."

Carol grinned at her. "Just a little gem from law enforcement."

Gloria smiled in return and Carol was struck with the difference it made in her. She obviously had a sense of humor, and her company when she was laughing and relaxed, rather than darkly brooding, would no doubt be rewarding.

"You have some questions?" said Gloria.

"How well do you know Fiona Brandstett?"

Gloria looked at her quizzically. "That's an odd question. Why do you ask?"

"Just for background," said Carol.

"It's really rather strange. You know, of course, that the Brandstetts are friends of Christine and Mitchell and that there's a business link with TTB Computing?" At Carol's nod she continued, "Fiona's a particular friend of Christine's, so when she went out of her way to be pleasant to me, I was suspicious about it—thought Christine was using her to spy on me because of Mitchell."

"And?"

"And it doesn't seem to be that at all. Fiona always chats with me if she comes into the office and we've had coffee a few times. Christine's never been mentioned."

"You don't think it is just straight friendship?"

Gloria grinned. "Come on!" she said, "Fiona Brandstett and Gloria Tyne as best friends? What a laugh!"

"So why?"

"Search me."

Carol asked a few more questions about Fiona, but it was obvious that Gloria was as puzzled as she by the close attention. She turned to Brett and Christine. "The letter from Brett Tait. How did Mitchell get hold of it?"

She shook her head. "I don't know. I didn't give it to him. I'd never seen it before."

"Did you get the impression Mitchell had found it himself—perhaps in his wife's things?"

"No, I'm sure someone gave it to him. I got the impression he was furious with whoever it was, but he never mentioned a name."

Carol said carefully, "Do you know if he was planning to confront Christine with it?"

"Christine? No. I thought he would certainly have it out with Brett first."

"Did he?"

Gloria was sardonic. "Don't ask me. You're the detective." Carol tilted her head and Gloria gave a reluctant smile. "No," she said, "I'm practically sure he didn't. I saw Brett a couple of times and there was no tension between them that I could see. Brett didn't act as though he'd been caught out and Mitchell was moody—but that's all."

"Why did Mitchell show the letter to you?"

"He was angry—he wouldn't have mentioned it otherwise, because it gave me ammunition to demand he leave Christine."

Carol knew this contradicted what Gloria had told Bourke. She said, "Had you been demanding that?"

Her tone resigned, Gloria said, "Yes, although I knew it was a waste of time. Mitchell wasn't about to break up his marriage. It had too many advantages for him. But I kept trying…"

She caught Carol's look. "Oh, yes—you're going to say I gave a different story to Detective Bourke. Funny, that—I just didn't feel like being a main suspect for the murder."

"I would have thought," said Carol, "you'd be more likely to murder Christine Tait than her husband."

Gloria was tightly amused at that. "What? And have the man I love arrested for his wife's murder? Give me a break, Inspector!"

During the hour and a half it took her to drive north to Pearl Beach, Carol went over the information the morning had provided. She wasn't altogether sure that Gloria hadn't given her a judicious mixture of truth and lies, but if so, distinguishing one from the other presented some problems.

Mark Bourke had also spent some of the morning interviewing and they had compared notes in a long telephone call. Turning over what he had told her, she tried to match the pieces in a puzzle that was only slowly taking shape.

Bourke's interrogation of Kurt had been short and sharp. After a hammering of pointed questions, Kurt had admitted he was still in love with Gloria and had some hopes that once she was over Mitchell's death she might return to him. He had said this quite frankly, seemingly oblivious to the thought that it might give him a strong motive to remove Mitchell permanently. Bourke had asked if Kurt knew that Mitchell's will gave control of the company to Gloria. Kurt had said he wasn't surprised and that it didn't make much difference to him. "His lip didn't actually tremble," Bourke had said to Carol, "but I can tell you, he wasn't overjoyed about the idea."

Bourke had also received the final report on the murder weapon: the blood traces did belong to Mitchell's rare AB blood type and therefore the knife was almost certainly used to kill him. A doorknock of the neighborhood by the local police hadn't uncovered anyone who had seen a person acting suspiciously near the stormwater drain. "Too much to hope for, anyway," Bourke had said cheerfully, adding, "And your question about the air-conditioning—it was given a complete overhaul about a month ago. It's an elaborate system, you know, but only the best for the Taits, eh?"

Carol remembered Bourke's tone with irritation. She felt he was still determined to pin the murder on Christine, and, although she knew him to be scrupulously fair, she had misgivings about his impartiality in this case. She also had to admit that Bourke must be thinking the same thing about *her*. She had pressing reasons to want Christine innocent—not the least being the chance of public exposure as a lesbian if there was a murder trial.

The traffic driving north was reasonably light and Carol enjoyed the highway's long swoops and curves through the spectacular landscape, an old land of wrinkled, weathered contours spread with a layer of scrub and trees. The road builders had left huge towering islands of ocher yellow sandstone to separate the north and south routes, and the pale gray road unwound beneath a luminous blue sky, the brooding cloud cover having been peeled back by high winds.

Pearl Beach had once been an isolated little place with a

few simple family shacks. Now it was the playground of those with ample finances and a taste for exclusivity. Situated on the ocean side of a fat finger of land jutting into Broken Bay, it was backed by the dense unspoiled bushland of a national park. Pearl Beach's narrow curving crescent of yellow sand was flanked by holiday houses that ranged from original wooden bungalows to garishly ostentatious edifices. The local council, possibly possessing a collective sense of humor, had named the streets with jewelry in mind—Diamond, Ruby, Crystal, Emerald.

And it had been at Pearl Beach that she and Christine had first made love.

She and Justin, together with another couple, had been guests of the Taits for a summer weekend. Early on Monday morning, Justin, Mitchell and the other couple, whose names Carol couldn't remember, had returned to Sydney, leaving herself and Christine to clean up the house and follow later in the day.

Tight with alarmed anticipation, unwilling to be alone in the house with Christine, she had suggested a swim before they began putting things in order. She could still remember Chris's amused, almost predatory glance as she agreed.

And when they returned to the house, salty and hot, Christine had said, "You can't avoid it any longer. You know we're going to make love, don't you?"

Carol had been trembling, not with guilt, not even with passion, but with delight at the promise of a new world. Christine's hands had been sure and her mouth demanding. Carol had gasped, "Chris, you've done this before, haven't you—with someone else?"

"With another woman? Yes, but never like this...never like this."

Carol could vividly remember the feverish shock of Christine's fingers within her, the rapacious appetite that gripped her, greedy for satisfaction, Christine's voice husky with passion— "Dearheart, yes. Come for me!"

And then touching Christine's avid body, exulting in the surge of rhythm that forced Chris to cry out…

Carol braked suddenly. She had almost missed the turnoff to Pearl Beach. Resolutely she pushed her memories aside. The past was the past. She had driven up here to help Christine— and that was all.

The Taits' house, one street back from the beach, was a reasonably modest weatherboard with a captivating garden of tree ferns and palms. Carol was determinedly poised when the door was opened to her, flicking a glance at Christine's tight white jeans and cobalt blue shirt, evading her welcoming embrace and walking through to the back of the house without ceremony.

Christine, following, said, "Are you angry with me?"

Carol turned to face her. "I'm angry with you—but mainly with myself. That kiss…it never should have happened."

"I suspect you won't want to hear this, but I love you and you're making me pay for a mistake that I've already paid enough for. Three years ago I should have left Mitchell and gone with you. You don't have to believe me, but I have never stopped loving you, never stopped wanting you…"

"Chris, please—"

Christine's voice was savage as she interrupted. "You've only known Sybil for a few months. You can't love her the way you love me. I don't care what you say, I know that's true!"

Carol walked remote and alone across Pearl Beach's slither

of pale sand. Christine had said she would rather stay and read and Carol was grateful to escape her for a while.

The arms of the little bay embraced the green water; one sleek yacht bobbed at anchor, its sails furled, a clump of superior people sitting nonchalantly on the stern tossing comments to each other. Small intent children played absorbing games with sand and water, larger ones cavorted in the modest surf.

She made her way along the rocks of the southern shore, making detours to avoid the flying hooks of novice fishers whose enthusiasm presented constant dangers of impalement to anyone passing by. The stone platform had weathered into fascinating patterns of tan, brown and cream; in one place the combination of red layers with underlying pale sandstone had created a rock rainbow cake and two-tone boulders.

Carol found a shelf of rock just below the tenacious gray-green vegetation of the upper headland and stretched out in the sun, shutting her eyes to let the world spin away. The water slapped pleasantly against the rock, kids shouted, seagulls provided distant shrieks and an appropriately gentle breeze blew the scent of salt and seaweed.

As she began to relax in the warmth, images began to form, shatter, reform. Christine's presence confused and disturbed her. All the painstaking effort over the last three years to build barriers as a protection against grief and longing had been a waste of time. Christine had simply smiled, kissed her once, and Carol's composure was shaken and her self-possession lost.

This was love? A turmoil of desires and emotions?

But love with Sybil was different. Her affection could be a comfort, a delight. Pictures danced behind Carol's closed eyes: Sybil smiling, her lips curling at the corners; the faint dusting of freckles across her nose; the way she ran her fingers though the red hair that curled into her graceful neck; her lightning change of moods; her willing body, ardent and ablaze.

"Tonight," said Carol aloud, "I'll see you tonight."

All the way back to the house she forced herself to concentrate on Mitchell's murder, rerunning conversations, looking for inconsistencies, trying to fit the pieces together to make a coherent whole. She paraded the suspects one by one, mentally trying out scenarios where each in turn played the major role of murderer. She ran the scene with Brett Tait starring, then Fiona Brandstett—and lastly she reluctantly gave Christine a chance to play principal actor.

With a jolt of surprise Carol realized she had walked the entire way back to the house oblivious to her surroundings. She frowned at the Volvo parked in the driveway, remembering that Christine had said she hadn't wanted anyone else here.

Christine was arguing furiously with someone in the kitchen. As Carol walked openly, but quietly, through the unlocked front door, Christine was saying vehemently, "I don't know what you expect me to do!"

"Chris, you promised me! You know what you said!"

"For God's sake, Fee! All right!"

Then, suddenly aware they were no longer alone, both women looked towards the hallway. Carol said pleasantly, "Hello, are you up for the day?"

Fiona Brandstett's eyes glittered with acrimony, a nerve was jumping in her cheek and her hands were clenched until her knuckles shone white. But her well bred voice was even. "Just calling in to see Chris for a moment."

Christine showed no sign of strain. She smiled at Carol as she said, "A nice surprise—Fee dropping in like this."

Sardonically amused, Carol deliberately looked Fiona over, noting the deceptively simple but undoubtedly expensive sundress and the imported high-heeled sandals. Fiona's skin was evenly tanned, her makeup perfect, her selection of a plain gold necklet exactly correct for the outfit. Probing for a sore spot, she said, "I suppose you expected to find Chris alone?"

Fiona had herself well in hand now. She both looked and sounded bored as she replied, "I didn't think about it." Then, to Christine, "I must go. I'd like to see you, soon."

The pause before the last word was subtle emphasis enough. Carol saw Christine's eyebrows lift fractionally. She said, "I'm up here for a couple of days. Call you when I get back."

Fiona hesitated, and, when Christine didn't move, said, "Come out to the car with me?"

Carol followed them to the front door. Fiona slammed the door of the car, Christine bent her head to hear a final sentence, then stood while Fiona backed out of the driveway and roared off down the street.

Carol, full of certain knowledge, was waiting. As Christine entered the house, Carol said conversationally, "How long has Fiona Brandstett been your lover?"

Chapter 10

Christine laughed. "Fee my lover? I can give you a comprehensive answer on that. She isn't, she hasn't been in the past and she never will be."

"She loves you."

"Carol, I can't control what people feel. Can you?"

Carol thought, I can't control what *I* feel, let alone anyone else. She said, "It's more than friendship."

Christine was unperturbed, opening the refrigerator and surveying the contents critically as she said, "What time is it? Too early for lunch?"

Carol went to change into jeans and a shirt—she felt vulnerable in a swimming costume—then she went to watch Christine prepare lunch. It was fascinating to observe her in a kitchen. She was a brilliant cook with a flair not only for preparation, but for presentation. Carol had often sat in the Taits' kitchen at Lindfield chatting to Christine as she chopped vegetables, made sauces, created elaborate deserts—all with a sure skill and economy of movement that was almost hypnotic.

Now, as Christine deftly prepared a simple salad that would look better, and somehow also taste better, than any similar offering from someone else, Carol began not to chat but to ask a series of searching questions.

"Has Fiona ever said she loved you?"

"Yes, but I let her down gently. Told her it was no go."

"She was happy to settle just for friendship?"

Christine considered the question. "Happy? No, not completely. But willing to continue as we had before—close friends."

"No doubt she knows about our affair."

Christine smiled at her affectionately. "I'm sure that's what encouraged her to finally say something to me about how she felt."

"Does John Brandstett know?"

A shrug. "I've no idea. He'd be furious if he did. John is terribly conscious of what his precious business associates think, not to mention everybody else in his circle."

She handed Carol a basket of bread rolls. "Let's eat outside. Since you were last here we've had a patio built out the back."

Carol said, "Was Fiona jealous of Mitchell?"

Frowning, Christine measured ingredients to make a dressing for the salad. "Probably. We didn't discuss it" She looked over to Carol. "Looking for a motive? Honestly, Carol, I don't know if Fiona could feel strongly enough to go ahead and murder someone—particularly Mitchell."

"Even if she did, it wouldn't get her you, would it?"

Christine shook her head. "No...but *you* can have me without lifting a finger."

135

Casually, Carol said, "Perhaps Fiona does feel strongly enough about you to be willing to give you an alibi."

Gray-blue eyes direct, Christine said, "I'm not lying about that Wednesday, Carol. I was with Fiona when Mitchell was murdered. Despite what the police may think, I didn't encourage Brett to kill his brother on my behalf. I don't know who did it and until you find out, I feel as though I'm in danger myself."

"Did Mitchell know about Fiona?"

The reply was unequivocal. "No. Absolutely not."

Carol said, "How about Brett? Does he know?"

Christine was growing impatient. "There's nothing to know!"

"Is he aware her feelings for you are rather more than friendship?"

Half-smiling at Carol's persistence, Christine said, "Dearheart, you're like a terrier! You just won't let go till you get what you want."

Carol smiled in turn. "Just answer the question, Chris."

"Brett resents the amount of time I spend with Fee." She looked at Carol, sighed in resignation, and said, "To be truthful, it's more than that. Brett knows how Fiona feels, and he's jealous. He won't believe me when I say on my side it's just friendship." She gave Carol a crooked smile. "He says it wasn't friendship with *you*, so why should it be with Fiona." She poured the dressing she had made into a cruet and handed it to Carol. "Hungry? Let's have lunch."

At the back of the cottage was a flagged sandstone patio with a stone balustrade over which arched a pergola hung with yellow flowering creepers, the whole area given privacy by high fences and ranks of luxuriant palms, umbrella trees and ferns. Seated in the dappled sunshine with the sound of the sea sighing in the distance, Carol wanted to blank out her mind and just enjoy the beauty of the day. Instead she said,

"The afternoon you two discovered Mitchell's body—who arrived at the house first, you or Brett?"

"I arrived a few seconds before he did. I was just turning off the engine when he pulled up behind my car."

"Does Brett have a key to your house?"

Christine shook her head. "Not unless Mitchell gave him one. It's possible, I suppose." She looked inquiringly at Carol. "Didn't you know some of the windows were unlocked? Mitchell had opened them. You wouldn't need a key to get in."

Carol thought of Mitchell's surprising lack of opposition to his murderer. It had been someone he had no idea would attack him. A friend? A brother? A woman?

"Chris, would you go through that Wednesday with me, please? Every detail."

Christine's account hadn't varied from her original one, and Carol hadn't expected that it would. What she was interested in was information about the finding of the body and Brett's reaction to the realization his brother was dead. Patient questioning elicited the same sequence of events that Brett had described.

Christine said, "Do we have to go over this again and again?"

"That's how it is. Somewhere, in all these words, is the key to the puzzle."

Despite the heat, Christine shivered. "I hate it," she said quietly, "I hate the questions and the suspicions…"

"Thanks, no more," said Carol as Christine went to pour wine into her glass. "I have to go soon."

"Stay the night."

"I can't."

Christine's voice was soft, compelling. "It's like it always was, Carol—you love me, and I love you."

Standing up abruptly, Carol went to lean on the stone balustrade and look out into the lushness of the garden. She was aware of Christine close behind her, but ignored the imperative to turn, continuing to examine, item by item, the color and shade before her.

Christine moved until she was standing directly behind Carol—pressed against her, pressed so closely Carol could feel Christine's hips, the zipper of her jeans, the heat of her body.

"Carol, stay still for me."

"What are you—"

"Shhh."

Carol shuddered as Christine slid her right hand around to rest gently across her stomach. She thought: I must move.

"It's all right, dearheart," whispered Christine against the nape of her neck, her fingers sliding under the band of Carol's jeans, tightly jammed against the quivering muscles of her stomach by the tension of the fabric.

Carol heard herself groan.

"It's all right," Christine said again.

Carol wanted to move, to push her away, to escape, but she was held by a ravenous appetite that yearned for the touch of her fingers.

Christine's other hand cupped her breasts, lightly grazing the material of her shirt, bringing her nipples erect to seek the burning brush of fingers.

Against her Carol could feel Christine's excited breathing, the pulsing of her body, the pounding of her blood. In turn, Carol felt all her desire gather, flood, flow in impatient pain.

Christine laughed softly, triumphant. She was deliberately slow, tantalizing, holding back the touch Carol tensed to feel, lifted her hips to achieve.

"Carol? Do you want it now?"

Knees locked, arms trembling, eyesight clouded with the craving of her eager body, Carol gasped, "Yes!"

Obediently, Christine's fingers plunged, stroked—building a rhythm of such intensity that Carol felt reality whirling into violent patterns of color and sound.

And when she couldn't bear it—couldn't bear to feel any more—she crested up and over into a shuddering ecstasy.

As Carol hung her head, moaning with the abatement of her passion, Christine whispered, close against her, "I love you, and I know you love me. You always will."

Chapter 11

Sybil sat in the beachside restaurant, chin on clenched fist, looking out through the rapidly fading light at the angry water. A sharply urgent wind was harrying the surface, raising its hackles in whitecaps and sending it growling onto the shore. A few determined people still braved the stinging sand on the beach but most had retreated, like Sybil, to view the souring evening behind the protection of glass.

She was early, having been restlessly anxious all afternoon. The sudden relief she felt when, through the plate glass doors, she saw Carol's car, made her suddenly aware of how much she had been preparing herself for disappointment.

Carol came walking briskly across the esplanade toward the restaurant. The wind was whipping her blonde hair across her face and she tossed her head impatiently to clear her eyes.

Sybil stared at her as though she wanted to imprint every detail in her memory. Her throat tightened with love and fear. She thought, How can I live without you?

She watched Carol's quick smile as someone opened the door for her. What was Carol thinking and feeling? And Christine…Could she hope to win against the combined force of Christine's sensual attractiveness and the store of shared memories?

Then she was abruptly angry with herself. What am I? she thought, some kind of wimp?

"Hi," said Carol, smiling.

She smiled in return. "You look great."

Sybil had rehearsed her words. She waited until they had ordered, then said, "Carol, I don't want to make any demands on you—"

"Make demands on me."

"What?"

The only sign of tension Carol showed was the nervous movement of her fingers as she twisted her black opal ring. She repeated, "I want you to make demands on me."

"Why?"

Carol sighed. "I don't know…" Their eyes met. Carol gave a wry smile. "Yes, I do. I'm trying to avoid responsibility for my own actions."

"What's happened between you and Christine?" Carol looked away.

Cold with certainty, Sybil said, "You've made love."

"Sybil, I…"

Sybil was terrified by the emotions that gripped her. In all her controlled existence she had never before realized the molten power love in all its manifestations could exert.

She thought, I can get up and leave—walk out on her. But what then? What would that resolve? She kept her voice steady by an act of will. "Are you going back to her?"

Carol's eyes met hers. "No." She looked away.

Any further reply was stopped by the arrival of their first course. Carol toyed with her oysters, Sybil stared at her prawns. The silence became unbearable. Carol said, "I wouldn't hurt you for the world…"

"Let's say, not deliberately."

"I never wanted any of this to happen."

Sybil was determined not to sound bitter but her tone was brittle as she said, "Am I supposed to wait around until you decide what you will or won't do?"

With a faint smile Carol said, "I don't think I can win, whichever way I answer that one."

Another silence. Sybil's thoughts were filled with what she wanted to say, but didn't dare—bitter, loving words.

By unspoken agreement they began to talk of safer, though more macabre, topics, as though they were merely friends, not lovers. Carol explained briefly how the investigation was progressing and answered Sybil's queries on how it could be established that the knife found was the one that had killed Mitchell.

"It's usually impossible to prove conclusively that a particular knife is the one used—what happens is that when the blood type matches and the wounds could have been made by that particular blade, then, on the balance of probabilities, it is the weapon. Fingerprints of the main suspect would help, of course, but in this case the knife's been carefully washed so there aren't any."

"Yet there are still traces of blood?"

Carol explained the helpful persistence of blood and how many murderers had been sure all traces had been removed, only to find scientific evidence irrevocably linking them to their victims.

"Wouldn't the person who killed Mitchell Tait have been covered in blood too?"

"Stab wounds don't usually cause much bleeding outside the body because the entry wound is a slit and the skin closes when the knife is withdrawn. In Mitchell's case there was a little more blood than usual but not enough to cause a problem to the murderer."

All at once Sybil felt the incongruity of calmly eating seafood and discussing the violent extinction of life. "This is horrible," she said.

"It is, but I suppose it's the way you learn to cope with things that could affect you so much if you let them…I couldn't do my job if I allowed myself to feel too much."

Bizarrely, Carol suddenly had a vision of Sybil murdered as Mitchell had been. An echo of the emotions she would feel in such a situation held her still.

Sybil said, "What's the matter?"

Carol shook her head. "Not a thing. Come on, darling, eat up—the waiter's hovering with a militant eye."

Following Carol's car home, Sybil lectured herself. Carol had said no when she had asked if she was going back to Christine. What more could she expect? She tried to imagine how she might feel in such a situation. Was it possible to love two people at the same time?

Sybil smiled wryly, thinking, My experience in love isn't much help…I've never cared about anyone really deeply until Carol.

They went together into the house and Sybil, looking at Carol, suddenly wanted to cuddle her and make her laugh. In just a few days Carol had lost weight and there was a strained set to her mouth.

"Coffee?" Carol asked.

As they went into the kitchen Sybil was filled with a

sudden delight just to be with her, alone. She seized Carol from behind as she was filling her ancient coffee percolator, hugging Carol's body tightly against her. Carol stiffened, and Sybil, feeling the taut rejection, slackened her arms and let her go.

"I'm sorry."

"Sybil, I…"

"It doesn't matter."

But, of course, it did. Carol had just come from Christine—from Christine's embraces—from making love in the languorous afternoon.

"Doesn't it worry you," said Sybil bitterly, "that you have this penchant for murderous women?"

"What?

"Well, Carol, let me present the evidence. *I* was the main suspect for Tony's murder. Christine is in the running for *her* husband's murder. Something about black widows attracts you, is that it?"

"Don't be ridiculous."

The telephone rang. Saved by the bell, thought Sybil.

She watched Carol's face change as she listened. She had come to know that abstracted look as Carol gazed, green eyes unfocused, at something no one else could see.

Replacing the receiver, Carol said, "That was about an alibi."

Sybil immediately thought of Christine. "Is one broken?" Carol looked at her with tired amusement. "Broken?" she said. "No. One's been created."

Chapter 12

Carol swore as the rain blew in under the carport. She hated wet weather and the leaden depression that it always brought her. In an effort to dispel her dejection she had selected a glowing tangerine dress but the vibrancy of the color only seemed to emphasize the pensive dolor of the day.

She and Sybil had slept in the same bed, careful not to invade the other's personal space. She had woken reluctantly to the damp and miserable day. Breakfast was endured. Each had tried to behave normally, but both were too aware of a hidden agenda in the most innocent remark. They had an awkward, fragmented, unsatisfying conversation where Carol neither said what she wanted to say, nor heard what she wanted to hear.

Carol called Brett with the irritated certainty that he

would be bubbling with enthusiasm. She was right; his voice rang with zest. "Carol! You heard? They've found her—the woman I had lunch with."

He had readily agreed to see her. "Let's meet. somewhere for coffee," he said, and Carol, remembering his ugly apartment and grubby office, had concurred.

Driving through the warm gray morning, the metronome of the wipers barely coping with the hammering rain, windows misting and the hazard of pedestrians rushing like lemmings across the road, did not improve her temper. Nor did thinking of Sybil's bitter question—Doesn't it worry you that you have this penchant for murderous women?

True, Sybil herself had been the main suspect for not one, but two killings. When Carol had first met Chris there was no question of murder—but now, seeing her again in the center of an investigation, Chris was surrounded by the crackling excitement of the chase. And she herself was filled with that emotional charge that came from outwitting, trapping, controlling someone who had stepped outside the bounds of normal behavior and taken another's life. Was that why she found Chris so compelling? Because she might be guilty of murder?

She grimaced as she faced the thought she had previously always pushed away. Perhaps, at some unconscious level, violence excited and attracted her. Perhaps the possibility that a woman had taken the final step of killing was a component in the magnetic force that had drawn her to both Sybil and Christine.

But she had been involved in several cases where the murderer was female. Surely she hadn't felt a tug of attraction each time? She smiled caustically. Perhaps she was selective, reserving her passion for those suspects whose intellects and bodies made them worthy of her attention.

She shook her head impatiently. How could she ever be

sure that she really understood her own motivations? It was too hard a question. There was no point in thinking about it.

Brett was already at the coffee shop when she arrived, sitting at a table by the window looking cheerily out at the damp umbrella carriers passing by.

He ordered coffee for them both, then hunched over the small table to share his relief and pleasure with her. "I'm sure you didn't believe me—no one did. But I was telling the truth and now you know I was. I couldn't have killed Mitchell because I wouldn't have had enough time to drive from Parramatta to Lindfield."

"So you and Christine are in the clear."

Brett's face clouded at the mention of her name. "I called Chris at Pearl Beach last night to tell her what had happened. I wanted to drive up right there and then, but she put me off. I don't know why she won't see me."

Carol said, "I spent part of the day there yesterday."

Brett looked at her keenly. "Was she alone, apart from you?"

"Most of the time. Fiona Brandstett called in for a while."

He pulled back his lips in derision, but said nothing. After a pause, Carol casually remarked, "Fiona seems rather intense about Christine."

"Carol, you're needling me. You know about it, don't you?"

"Yes. Chris told me yesterday."

Brett was shaking his head. "How could she—with Fiona? *You*, I understand. You're beautiful. But Fiona…"

"Chris says it's totally one-sided."

Brett's face was bitter. "Does she? That's not the impression I have. They're lovers." He put his cup down so savagely that coffee slopped into the saucer. "Fiona'd kill for Chris, you know. She'd do anything."

Carol smiled gently. "Ah, Brett," she said, "but that's what *you* said in your letter isn't it? That you'd do anything for Chris, anything at all?"

He shrugged. "The difference is I wrote that in the heat of the moment some time ago when I was drunk and Chris had just kissed me. Fiona's having an affair with her right now. I'm sure of it. God! Haven't you seen the way she watches Chris? She is obsessive."

"Obsessive or not, why would she murder Mitchell?"

"Oh, come on, Carol! What do you think he'd have done about Fiona Brandstett? He'd have crucified her. And made sure she never saw Chris again.

"Do you think he suspected there was something between them?"

Brett almost sneered as he said, "Well, at least you and Chris had sensitized him to the possibility."

She remained unruffled by his tone. "So Mitchell did have suspicions?"

"Of course. He must have!"

Hearing the excited conviction in his voice, she said, "You'd like it to be Fiona, wouldn't you?"

"Damn right, I would!"

"Why?"

"Because she's a bitch. She's done her best to turn Chris against me—tried to persuade her that *I* killed Mitchell."

"What's her reason for doing that?"

"Jesus! I don't know. Maybe to cover herself. Maybe to get me out of the way. Take your pick."

"You realize," said Carol, "that if Fiona killed Mitchell then Christine doesn't have an alibi."

He didn't reply. In the silence Carol considered Fiona Brandstett in the role of murderer. She was sardonically amused with the thought that if Sybil's comment of this morning had weight, she should now be feeling the stirrings of desire for Fiona.

Brett saw the slight twitch of her lips. "Funny, is it?" he said viciously. "You can laugh now, but you'll be up to your neck in it if Chris is charged. Fiona—*she'd* keep things quiet. But I, for one, will make sure everyone knows you have a personal ax to grind if Chris goes to trial. You can be sure of that!"

"Heavens, Brett," said Carol with an ironic smile, "how having an alibi does make one ungrateful. I gather you don't feel you need my help now—is that right?"

He scooped back his hair with his habitual gesture. "Look, just find out who did it, okay? I know it isn't me, and it can't be Chris. You work it out, Carol."

Mark Bourke looked up from his desk with a grin. "Carol Ashton," he said, "the very woman I want, indeed, *need* to see!"

"How flattering," said Carol, returning his smile with real affection. Were she in Mark's position, she suspected she would be most reluctant to have a superior unofficially involved, but although he obviously felt awkward at times, he was clearly pleased to have her help and opinions.

His office was as neat as the list he had drawn up on a whiteboard. They stood together and studied the names: Christine Tait, Brett Tait, Gloria Tyne, Kurt Boardman, Fiona Brandstett, John Brandstett and Rosie Lee.

"I'm bloody sure one of them did it," said Bourke. "I know Christine, Fiona and Brett have alibis but I can't believe they're as firm as they look."

Carol said, "Let's go through them."

"Okay, starting at the bottom we have Rosie Lee. Somehow I can't visualize her sticking a knife through Mitchell's ribs, though in these days of rampant feminism, who knows what might happen. She certainly had the opportunity to follow him home, argue about her job, then dispatch him—but where did she get the knife? It's hard to believe that on the way she just popped into a hardware store on the off chance she'd have the opportunity to stab him."

He pointed to John Brandstett's name. "He's got an alibi of sorts, but the secretary who says he was in his office at the vital time has a brain like a gnat."

Carol raised her eyebrows so he elaborated. "Brandstett's personal secretary is a charming girl whose best features are not intellectual. If you ask me, she'd have a lot of trouble deciding what day it was, let alone whether or not her boss was around at any given time."

"Does she remember the call from Mitchell Tait cancelling the appointment he had with Brandstett?"

"Nope. She doesn't remember much of anything, but she smiles a lot."

Carol indicated Fiona Brandstett's name. Bourke pursed his lips. "Bit of an outsider in the field, but could surprise. I have a feeling about that alibi she and Christine Tait share…"

Carol moved uncomfortably, finding the words difficult to say. "Mark, I've been told that there's a possibility Fiona Brandstett and Christine Tait are lovers—or it may be that it's totally one-sided, in that Fiona feels strongly, but Christine doesn't."

He was silent, squinting at the names on the board. Carol suddenly realized that he was, of all things, embarrassed. She said, "What's the matter?"

He turned to her soberly. "I feel a bit awkward, knowing you and Christine Tait were…close."

"Forget it. It's not important any more."

"Carol, I don't think we can forget it. It could be an issue—"

"Mark, I really don't want to discuss this."

Bourke cleared his throat, businesslike again. "Right," he

said, "so that means there's a possibility Christine and Fiona agreed to alibi each other and jointly, or singly, killed the inconvenient husband."

"Kurt Boardman?"

Bourke rubbed his chin. "Don't know about Kurt. He nurses a surprisingly intense passion for Gloria and I think, underneath all the Mr. Nice Guy sales persona, is someone who hated and despised Mitchell Tait. His situation is rather like Rosie Lee's. He could just about make it to Mitchell's place to kill him but the timing could be a bit tight."

"Mark, I've had some thoughts about the time of death. When we finish this I'd like to discuss it."

He looked at her with interest, but obediently went on with the list of suspects. "Okay, now we have Gloria Tyne, who is, I have to say, rather growing on me."

"In what way?"

Bourke grinned at Carol's dry tone. "Let's just say I think I'm beginning to appreciate her rather elusive charms. Now that she's relaxing her guard I get the impression of a much more interesting person behind the wild genius front."

"It's time you settled down," said Carol, straight-faced.

Bourke gave her a mocking world-weary look and continued. "On the face of it Gloria is probably our best bet. She has opportunity and motive and rather incautiously said she'd like to see Mitchell dead. That, however, worries me. She's hardly a fool, and to threaten someone one day, and murder him the next, is pretty foolish behavior."

"You know as well as I do, Mark, that the most intelligent person can lose control and do something quite uncharacteristically stupid."

He nodded agreement. "Do you think Brett Tait's intelligent?" he said.

Carol shrugged. "He's not dumb. Why?"

"I just wonder if he believes anyone would accept his story

about the love letter being just a drunken slip of the pen. And if he asked himself why Christine kept it so her husband could conveniently find it."

"Gloria said she had the impression someone had actually given it to Mitchell."

"Who? The person with the most to gain would be Gloria herself."

"What about Fiona Brandstett?"

Bourke cocked an eyebrow. "Breaking up the marriage so she could collect the delectable Christine?"

Carol shrugged. "It might be possible."

"It could have been Christine herself in a Look-your-brother-loves-me-what-do-you-think-of-that sort of way."

"Speaking of Brett, I saw him this morning, and he's brimming with confidence. I gather his alibi looks okay."

"Checked it out myself. The sales rep he chatted up at McDonald's is perfectly genuine. She's only been in Sydney a few weeks and there's no connection between her and Brett Tait at all. I'd say he's home, sweet."

Carol said, "So that blows your theory that Christine used him as a proxy to kill her husband."

Bourke sighed. "Sure does." He grinned at her. "That's why, Carol, I was so pleased to see you...I was wondering if you had any particularly bright ideas."

Carol didn't return his smile. "I think I have," she said. Before she could go on Bourke was called to the door of his office. He conferred with the officer for a few moments, then came back to Carol, his face grim.

"Fiona Brandstett's just been taken to St. Vincent's Hospital," he said. "But she was dead on arrival."

Chapter 13

Fiona had been found by one of the occupants of the other units in the block, huddled at the bottom of the last flight of stairs leading to the pool. One slip-on leather sandal had been left lying forlornly on a step halfway down; the other was by her body.

"Accident?" said Bourke to Carol as they stood on the artificial grass damp from the rain that had been falling in dismal sheets intermittently all morning.

Carol looked over at the pool where Fiona would never swim again. "I don't think so," she said decisively.

"So someone pushed her, tripped her or picked her up and threw her, to break her neck?"

"Yes," said Carol, "but I think we'll have a hard time proving it."

Bourke gazed reflectively at the palms and the harbor beyond. "Why would anyone go swimming in the rain?"

"Why not? You get wet anyway. Besides, Fiona Brandstett swam every day. Had a set exercise routine."

Bourke turned to a junior detective standing attentively nearby. "Ferguson, check everyone in the block and the neighbors on each side. I want to know if anyone saw or heard anything and also if Mrs. Brandstett went down to the pool at the same time each day."

Carol said, "Are you sure she was going down—maybe she was coming up *after* her swim. Was her costume wet?"

Bourke gave her an appreciative grin. "Ferguson," he said, "you heard Inspector Ashton. All the details on the swimming, eh?"

Carol hadn't liked Fiona Brandstett, but she was disturbed and saddened by her death. So much energy put into looking good, keeping fit—only to have it dashed away in one violent moment.

She sat at home doodling absently on a piece of paper, drawing circles around names. Sybil was out and the house was quiet and comfortable. She gazed thoughtfully at Jeffrey, who was washing behind his ears. She had been told as a little girl that this action heralded rain. "Stop that, Jeffrey," she suggested. He gave her a superior look and continued his ablutions.

Rain made her think of Fiona's swimming costume. The delay before it was examined meant that it had had time to dry, so until the medical report was available there was no way of telling if she had died earlier on the way to the pool, or later on the way back. Nobody remembered seeing her swimming that morning, but since it was raining for much of the time, this was not surprising.

But who would want Fiona dead anyway? Brett had made no secret of the fact he disliked her intensely because he believed she was Christine's lover, but was that enough motive to break her neck?

Detective Ferguson had discovered two things of interest. The first related to the schedule Fiona kept. She came down to the pool at different times, depending on whether she was going to sunbathe or not, but once she was there she always swam twenty laps of the pool before lunch, usually finishing before one.

The second item was that John Brandstett and Fiona had had a violent argument that morning—so violent that their neighbor below had complained, and been sworn at by Brandstett. The subject of the argument wasn't clear and Bourke had reported that John Brandstett was too upset by his wife's sudden death to be interviewed at the moment.

John Brandstett. Christine had said he would be furious if anyone in his circle of friends and business acquaintants found out his wife had lesbian tendencies…But would he fling her down the stairs to keep it quiet?

She wrote Gloria and Kurt's names and joined them with a large circle. Kurt seemed to have no connection with Fiona other than a casual acquaintance. Fiona had cultivated a friendship with Gloria, but this was almost certainly because it suited Fiona to be in proximity to Mitchell's lover—but was it at Christine's instigation, or was it for herself?

Christine? Fiona loved her, was obviously jealous and was making demands Chris was not prepared to meet—a difficult situation perhaps, but surely not one with murder as its solution.

When Fiona died, where had they all been? Bourke had demanded extra staff, moving quickly to check people out before they could have heard of Fiona's death. John Brandstett was in his office, but, as Bourke said with a grin, "It's that girl again, Carol—she *thinks* he was in the office most of the morning, but she's really not absolutely sure."

Christine was still at Pearl Beach when contacted. Brett was calling on prospective customers (Carol wondered if he had stopped for a hamburger and a timely chat) and Gloria said she and Kurt had spent the whole morning at her house working uninterrupted on strategic planning for the company.

"Carol?"

She stood, startled. "Chris? What're you doing here?"

"I've just driven from Pearl Beach. Have you heard? Fiona's dead!"

"Yes, I know."

Christine seized her by both elbows. "Don't you understand, Carol! She gave me my alibi for Mitchell's death...and now she's dead herself."

Christine's lips were trembling. The sensual line of her mouth was vulnerable and appealing. Carol said, "It's all right—"

"It's not all right! She was my friend and someone's killed her."

Carol freed herself and took her hands. "Calm down. It could have been an accident."

"Do you believe that?"

"I don't know."

Christine was dissolving into tears. "I can't take this. I feel someone's out to get me...to destroy me..."

"You're not thinking clearly."

"Please," said Christine. She put her arms around Carol and rested her wet cheek against Carol's face. Carol held her carefully, remotely.

There was a sound. Carol looked up to see Sybil standing in the doorway, blankly watching. Then, expressionless, she turned away.

156

Releasing Christine, Carol said, "Sybil, wait. It isn't—"

Sybil said over her shoulder, "Isn't what? Isn't serious? Or isn't what I think?"

Carol's voice was quiet. "Is there anything I can say or do that will change your mind?"

"No."

"When will I see you?"

Sybil put the overnight bag down and stood looking at the floor. She said, "I'll call you...tomorrow."

"I don't know your address or telephone number." With a shadow of a grin, Sybil said, "And you call yourself a detective."

She jotted it down and handed it to Carol. "It's Sally's place. I'll be there for the next few days."

"You don't have to go."

"I do."

Without Sybil the house seemed empty and sad. Even Jeffrey looked disconsolate. Carol felt as though she were enclosed in a plastic bubble, protected for a while from the sharp sting of loss.

Carol had to press the security buzzer several times before Brandstett's harsh voice crackled from the speaker. "Whoever you are, get out."

"It's Carol Ashton."

He swore. She said, "I believe your wife was murdered—but not by you."

There was a pause, then the lock on the security door was released. Carol rode up in the shiny metal elevator, her mind full of images of Fiona alive and imperious. All that poise and pride shattered by one violent push.

Brandstett was half-drunk, red-eyed and unsteady on his feet. He slammed the front door and then lurched back to the glaring brightness of the main room, obviously expecting her to follow. He glared at her, bellicose. "Murder—there's no murder. She fell. Accident." Seizing a bottle of whiskey, he slopped some into a glass and then slumped into a chair.

Seating herself opposite him, she said, "Is it true that Fiona and Christine were lovers?"

He swung his heavy head to focus on her face. "What?" He sounded almost absent-minded.

She repeated the question.

He took a large mouthful of the whiskey, then sighed, letting the truculence drain out of him. "This morning..." He paused, wiping his eyes with the back of his hand. "This morning we argued about it. Didn't do any good."

Carol wondered if his reddened eyes were as much from tears as whiskey. She asked quietly, "How long have you known about them?"

Brandstett's swollen face flamed. "I don't know! I suspected. Fiona would have walked across water for Chris, she wanted any crumb Chris threw her. But I didn't know for sure till this morning. Fiona told me."

Carol thought, What a perfect scenario for murder. She said, "Why did you try to blackmail me into keeping quiet? What did you think Fiona had said to me?"

Reaching over to grab the whiskey bottle, Brandstett slopped liquor down the front of his shirt. His whole attention caught on the stain, he brushed ineffectually at it. Obviously his consumption of alcohol would soon render him comatose, so Carol pressed the question upon him again.

"She was jealous! Christ! She was so jealous of you and Chris. When she was face to face with you, I was sure she'd say something stupid, challenge you. Demand you leave Chris alone. Something like that."

"But what if Fiona *had* said that to me? Why would that be a problem?"

He was suddenly fired with a drunken energy, struggling to his feet and swaying over her. "If she said she was a queer—you wouldn't keep it quiet, would you? Everyone'd know."

Carol's tone was dry. "You were worried about a scandal?"

"Not just that. Then you'd have a reason for her to kill Mitchell."

Carol stood, forcing him to move back. "And did she? Did Fiona murder Mitchell?"

He snorted in derision. "Kill Mitchell? How could she? When Mitchell died…" He stopped, his face contorting. "When Mitchell died she and Chris were here, making love."

"Are you sure of that?"

"Told me that this morning. Almost the last thing she said to me." He sat down slowly, putting his face in his hands. "Now get out."

Carol felt a mixture of pity and distaste as she complied.

Chapter 14

Morning: a new day, washed clean by yesterday's rain and brightly shining.

Last night Carol had discussed the case with Bourke, sifting through the evidence, testing her ideas and suspicions. Then she had gone to bed and slept deeply, dreamlessly. And during that sleep pieces of the puzzle had realigned, flipped over, clicked into place.

She was suddenly resolved. The will power that had driven her to overcome all the formidable obstacles in her career was reasserting itself, waking and stretching within her. She had made a decision of resonating importance.

She wrote a short letter to Sybil, pausing after the first words, then swiftly writing through to the end.

She called Bourke. "Mark? It's Carol. I think I have it. But proof—that's another matter. If Fiona had lived we could have broken the alibis. There's no possibility she left anything in writing?"

Bourke sounded tired. "She wasn't the dear diary sort, unfortunately."

"I think you should pick up Brett Tait. When I spoke to him yesterday he was cocky and secure because he thinks he's protected by an alibi. Take that away from him, and I think he'll break."

There was mild protest in Bourke's voice. "Carol, we don't have the proof."

"Mark, I'm coming in."

"If you stay out of it—"

"I can't."

"Carol, if you get involved and it comes to an arrest, you know there's no way I can protect you."

"Without me you probably won't have an arrest."

"We'll find a way."

"Come on, Detective Bourke. You know I'm your best chance, don't you?"

His voice was resigned. "If you say so, Inspector."

Carol positioned her car carefully in the Taits' drive, sat still for a moment, then said, "I'm going in now."

Christine was surprised, but pleased, to see her. Carol said without ceremony as they walked down the hall, "You should know they've arrested Brett for Mitchell's murder."

Stopping abruptly, Christine said, "Brett killed Mitchell? But he has an alibi."

"Oh, he does, but it's for the wrong time." She moved past Christine through the doorway into the room where Mitchell had died. "Can we sit in here?"

Christine followed her slowly. "I don't understand."

Carol sat in one of the pale leather chairs near the elaborate fireplace. She waited until Christine was also seated, then said, her tone clinical, "You know Brett desperately needs money to keep his business afloat. And he wants you. Will do anything to get you. Isn't that true?"

"I've never been interested in him!"

"No? But you made love with him. That was enough to persuade him he had a chance."

Christine sounded almost indignant. "Only once. That's all. I'd had too much to drink and Mitchell was away…"

Ignoring her explanation, Carol continued, "Having decided to kill his brother, Brett was smart enough to realize he needed some kind of alibi. Even if no one else knew about your affair, the two hundred thousand he was going to inherit would give him a motive."

"Carol, this is ridiculous. Brett would never hurt Mitchell."

"So he began to read up on forensic science. I don't want to bore you with too many details, but basically he discovered some interesting facts about dead bodies. Firstly, they cool at a steady rate, so when the temperature of the corpse is put in an equation that includes the temperature of the surroundings, an estimate can be made of the number of hours elapsed since the person died. Secondly, the stiffening of the muscles—rigor mortis—also runs to a timetable, starting within five hours of death and spreading progressively through the body, so that it, too, can give an indication of the time life ceased."

Christine's face was twisted with distaste. "Is all this necessary?"

"I want you to understand, Chris, why neither you nor Brett has an alibi."

"Me? It's Brett we're talking about."

"It is. So, now that Brett knows something about how the time of death is estimated, he investigates further, and he discovers a way to manipulate the evidence to give himself an alibi."

Christine was watching her in solemn concentration. Carol said, "Perhaps this sounds incredible, but you must realize that Mitchell's murderer was clever and determined."

"Go on."

"Brett has a plan. All he has to do is carry it out, gambling that he won't be noticed coming and going from your house. It's a reasonable chance to take—your neighbors value privacy. These are the steps Brett takes. He picks a day he knows you'll be away—and Wednesday will do, since you always have lunch with Fiona and then play tennis. He buys the knife he will use. He calls Mitchell and arranges to meet him at home. My guess would be that Brett told him it was about you and not to mention it to anyone because it was a private matter."

Christine was rubbing her fingers together. "Can you prove any of this?" she said.

Carol continued, "We don't know yet if Brett spent the hour or so before Mitchell died arguing with him, or if he waited until the last moment to enter the house, but whichever it was, he had to kill Mitchell by noon in order to give himself time to clean up and get to Parramatta. After he stabbed his brother, he washed the knife in the kitchen sink, turned the central air-conditioning system on to full heat and left to get rid of the murder weapon. He drove around until he found a quiet suburban street, held the knife in something to make sure no fingerprints were on it, and dropped it down the stormwater drain."

"I don't believe any of this."

Carol raised an eyebrow. "It gets better," she said. "Brett drives to Parramatta to find someone he can use as an alibi if it turns out to be necessary. He chats up a girl, making sure he'll be remembered, then drives back to Lindfield, arriving well before the time he is to meet you. He parks in a nearby street, goes into the house, which is, of course, stiflingly hot, and turns the air conditioning system full on the cooling cycle so that the temperature in the house will be brought down to near normal for the day."

She gestured to the rug in front of the fireplace. "Perhaps he comes in to look at Mitchell lying here on the floor. Then, just before you're due to arrive home he turns the air conditioning off, goes back to his car and waits to drive in behind you as though he's just arrived."

Christine shook her head. "I don't understand how all this works. What are you saying?"

"I'm saying that Brett killed Mitchell somewhere around noon, but the excellent air conditioning system installed in your house delayed the body's loss of heat considerably, so that the estimated time of death was put at one o'clock, not twelve. Of course, the use of heat did provide one unfortunate problem—as it speeds up rigor mortis, Brett had to have the body discovered before rigor was established, so he had a tight time frame in which to operate."

Christine rubbed her forehead. "Brett's going to say I asked him to do it for me. That we were in it together."

"I don't believe that," said Carol.

Christine looked up. Smiled. "Don't you?" she said.

Sybil looked at the envelope with Carol's distinctive writing. She turned it over in her hands, unwilling to open it. She wanted to shut herself off from the pain, the excuses, the explanations. Better to be alone than to feel like this.

Slowly, she opened the letter.

Christine said, "Fiona? Did Brett kill Fiona?"

"They hated each other."

"Yes."

"Because of you."

Christine's voice was peevish. "I didn't ask them to love me!"

"You made sure they did, and to tie each of them to you, to make the knot secure, you made love with both Brett and Fiona, didn't you?"

Christine hesitated, then said, "I can never lie to you, Carol, but Fiona and Brett, they meant nothing to me."

"Never lie to me? Chris, you've rarely told me the truth!"

Sybil's eyes were on Carol's letter, re-reading the lines.

Darling,

For me there have been two kinds of love.

The love I had for Chris was overwhelming—almost like a sickness—full of passionate emotion, but, if I can explain it this way, turning in on itself.

The love I have for you contains passion—but also laughter and friendship and a generosity that makes me want to give something back to the world, not hide it in myself.

In all the ways I might ever hope to, I love you.

Carol

Carol said, "Fiona was obsessed with you, but the first time you made love with her was the day Mitchell died."

"Why would you think that?"

"Yesterday morning she and her husband had a violent argument. Fiona told him she had finally made love with you the Wednesday of the murder."

Christine stared at her, stood, moved to lean against the

mantlepiece. "What does it matter, anyway?"

"It was to buy her cooperation."

"I don't know what you mean."

Carol examined the face she had known so well for so long. Chris looked the same—the familiar curve of her lips, the dimple in her chin, her wide blue eyes—but the pattern had a subtle change. In some way she was a stranger.

Carol said calmly, "You know I know, don't you?"

Christine raised her eyebrows in an unspoken query.

"All the things I said Brett did...it was *you*."

Christine stood at the fireplace looking down at Carol, a slight frown on her face.

Carol thought, You're so sure of me, Chris.

"I want to trust you."

There it was! The decision. Carol gave her a faint smile. "You can. Tell me."

"Can you really understand what it was like to be married to Mitchell, especially after you went away? He was crude, he was demanding. Yes, I know what you're going to say—I chose to stay with him. I did. But he changed. He didn't trust me. And he started the affair with Gloria Tyne. He was a bastard, Carol."

"Was that enough reason to kill him?"

"It wasn't just one reason—how could it be? I wanted a divorce, to be free, but he wouldn't let me go...I knew he'd tie up the property settlement in court, make sure I had to fight for every cent. And there were the threats he made over Fiona. He hated you, but Fiona he despised. He was violent and unpredictable and I was frightened of him."

Carol couldn't look at Christine any longer. She stared down at her hands, conscious of the tremor in her fingers. "Tell me how it happened."

"Carol, it was horrible. So much worse than I thought it would be. When I planned it, everything was so neat and exact. And it all worked, just as I had visualized it—except the way he died."

"Mitchell wasn't alarmed—to see you with a knife?"

Christine was speaking faster than usual, as though anxious to explain but unsure of the reception she would get. "When he came home I was working in the kitchen. I'd told him on the phone that Brett was forcing himself on me and that he was insisting on coming to see me that morning. I said I was frightened of what Brett might do. A few days before I'd given him the letter Brett wrote me—said how upset I was about it—so Mitchell believed me. I took the phone in the kitchen off the hook so he couldn't ring out and I started chopping up vegetables with the knife I had bought weeks before. It was a beautiful knife, Carol, weighted just right, and so easy to use. When I knew it was time I walked into the front room holding the knife and wearing a waterproof apron—though, as it turned out, I didn't really need it."

There was a brown stain on the rug where Mitchell had fallen. Carol's mind held a vivid picture of his body lying at Christine's feet. "Did he realize what was happening?"

Christine shook her head. "Only at the very last. He'd lashed himself into a fury waiting for Brett to arrive and when I came into the room he accused me of leading Brett on. He didn't even seem to notice the knife as he came over, threatened me…"

"You're not thinking of claiming self-defense, are you?"

"But dearheart, it won't come to that. They have Brett."

Carol's voice was calm and interested. "And then what happened next?"

"I stabbed him. I had to, having gone so far. You see that, don't you? I held the knife with both hands, and jabbed it up hard, right under his ribs. It was so strange. Mitchell just stood there, looking shocked. He couldn't believe it. He stared at me, said something, then fell. It only took a moment, and he was gone."

Carol looked up at Christine, unspeaking. Oh, Chris, she thought. Once I risked everything to have you. Now…

Christine moved to touch Carol's shoulder. "Dearheart, you do understand—I'm sure you must. I had to do it. There was no other way."

Carol cleared her throat. "I understand, Chris."

Satisfied, Christine resumed her seat in the chair opposite. "It was all as you said, Carol. It was clever of you to work it out. How did you do it? Why did you suspect it was me?"

"Such little things. One was that Brett noticed you turned the air conditioning system on when the two of you walked into the house, yet when the police arrived it was off, and you said it hadn't been on all day."

Nodding, Christine said, "I thought the house was still too hot. It had to be much closer to the outside temperature. And afterward, Brett was so upset when we found Mitchell that he didn't notice anything I did. I opened the windows and turned off the air conditioning just before the police arrived."

"Another thing was when Fiona said that you were early to her place for lunch—in all the years I've known you, you've never been on time, let alone early. And then Brett mentioned you surprised him by being on time at Lindfield."

"Yes, he nearly caught me. I thought I had plenty of time, because he knows I'm always a bit late so he doesn't hurry. But you know how I am—I meant to be out and sitting in my car as though I'd just drawn up there, but somehow I nearly didn't make it before he arrived. Actually, I thought for a moment he'd seen me coming out the front door."

"I'm sure he did."

"He didn't say anything."

"No. He's been protecting you. That's why he's been trying to see you."

Christine shrugged. "They won't believe anything Brett

says, now he's been charged with murder." She suddenly became earnest, leaning forward to persuade. "You know Brett hated Mitchell. He was so jealous of Mitchell's success. He would have killed him himself if he'd had the guts."

"And he was in love with you."

Christine dismissed that with a gesture of contempt. "Love? Brett wouldn't know what it was." "But Fiona Brandstett would."

"Fiona! She was so bloody intense."

Carol's tone was mildly ironic. "Surely an advantage when you needed her to provide you with an alibi. She was obviously willing to lie, not only about the time you arrived at her place, but about the time you left. That had to be much earlier, in order to give you time to cool the house down before Mitchell's body could be discovered."

"I didn't want to have to rely on Fiona—I couldn't trust her, not the way I can trust you."

Carol looked away from Christine's sincerity. She thought of Fiona dying in the dismal gray of a rainy day. "Was it easy to persuade Fiona to help you?"

"Easy? Yes, it was easy. She wanted to believe me when I told her I was sure Brett had killed Mitchell. I said Brett was jealous, that I'd turned him down for her, and that meant he would destroy me if he could, so I needed an alibi. Fiona wanted Brett to be guilty of murder. He was a rival and she hated him."

"And after that she started making demands on you?"

Shrugging in distaste, Christine said, "Fiona wanted me body and soul, just for herself. At first, when we were friends and I realized she was falling in love with me, I encouraged it. I suppose you wonder why. So do I, sometimes, but it amused me and I was bored. And it was a challenge to see how far she'd go. After all, she was top of the social tree, so sure of herself, so in control of her life…"

"You made love with her the day of Mitchell's death to seal the bargain."

There was a note of protest in Christine's voice. "It didn't mean anything to me."

Carol said mildly, "It's better for you that she's dead."

"Carol! You don't think I killed Fiona too?"

Carol said, "Fiona's death could have been an accident."

"It was!"

"But Chris, you did see her, didn't you?"

Christine stood up and began to pace in front of the fireplace. It was the first real agitation she had shown and Carol tensed at this crack in the smooth surface of her facade.

"Fiona rang me at Pearl Beach. She was wild because I'd asked you up there but hadn't invited her. She got more and more upset, and threatened me. Unless I saw her straight away, she'd go to the police about my alibi."

Christine's tone had turned persuasive as she justified herself. "Fiona wanted more from me than I could ever give. She wanted to suck me dry. She'd never let me go."

"You drove down from Pearl Beach…"

"Yes. She was alone, of course. I tried to placate her, but she was making the most ridiculous demands. You know, she was actually willing to leave John for me!"

A flash of bitter amusement filled Carol. She crushed the caustic words that rose in her mouth: Is that so amazing? *I* left Justin for you!

Christine was speaking rapidly, eager to explain. "We walked down the stairs together, arguing. Fiona wouldn't miss her precious swim, even for me. She was like a stranger, hissing furious accusations at me."

"It would be easy to push her."

Christine said, "Do you think I would do that?"

"You had to protect yourself."

A pause. Christine said, "She slipped—I swear she

slipped—but I'd taken a wrench from my car's tool kit, just in case."

Carol's lips tightened. Christine was suddenly shouting, "Don't judge me, Carol! Fiona was blackmailing me! She deserved everything she got!"

Carol stood. It was over. The listening device under her jacket had recorded everything that the monitoring Bourke needed to hear. From this morning's briefing she knew that Ferguson and Hardy would now be approaching to cover the front of the house, O'Neill the rear—all of them under Bourke's command. Yes, it was over. Everything was over.

She looked down at the stain Mitchell's blood had made on the rug. "I'm sorry, Chris."

"Sorry? What do you mean?"

"You can't really expect me to ignore what you've told me."

"But I do, Carol! I wouldn't have told you anything if I didn't trust you!"

Uselessly, she offered reason in the face of insanity.

"You've killed two people, Chris."

"They made me do it! Why won't you understand that?"

She shook her head, looking away so she couldn't see Christine's contorted face. "No, Chris. It's over."

The silence should have alerted her. As it was, she caught a flash of gleaming metal. There was an instant to realize that Christine had snatched the brass poker from the fire irons beside the black marble mantlepiece—then the room fragmented as the blow fell.

The rough texture of the rug was against her cheek. She saw, with extraordinary clarity, the splatter of her bright red blood forming new patterns. And Christine's shoes.

She tried to concentrate. Somewhere—it seemed far away—a voice was screaming, "It's your fault! It's your fault! I can't let you betray me!"

Time was stretching. Everything happened slowly,

deliberately. Christine will never hurt me, she had promised Mark Bourke. She realized she was going to die. She tried to raise an arm to protect her head, but her body didn't obey her. With disassociated interest she watched Christine balance herself and raise the poker with both hands.

She was calmly astonished to feel no pain. She wondered remotely if she would feel this final blow.

Christine had stopped screaming. There was silence as the poker, shining in its power, began to descend.

Carol stared at the warm glow of the metal, at Christine's intent face. Then there was a sudden sharp volley of noise that echoed and re-echoed in her head. Christine's graceful movement was broken as she opened her mouth in seeming surprise. Then her body twisted and she fell back out of sight.

Carol was puzzled. She tried to frown, but was too weary. She closed her eyes.

She could hear someone shouting for an ambulance. She identified the person. Mark Bourke. A sudden blinding pain flooded her head. She heard a groan, wondered at its source, then realized that it was her voice.

There was an agonizing vibration of footsteps and then Bourke's voice, close above her. He touched her face gently. "Don't move. It'll only be a few moments."

She forced her eyes open. Bourke was bending over her and from the unfamiliar perspective his face was subtly alien. He was white and sweating, his mouth a straight line of tension.

She knew there was a question she needed to ask. But she shut her eyes and let herself sink into the tepid darkness.

No pastel shades diluted the antiseptic white cube of the hospital room. A shaft of early morning sunlight slanted obliquely through the window, bringing with it the scents of warm spring air. Through the door filtered hospital sounds—busy footsteps, the clink of metal, professionally cheerful nursing voices making bracing comments.

She lay inert, too fatigued to turn her bandaged head, too remote to want to be touched by emotion. A headache hammered relentlessly inside her skull. Although she closed her eyes and willed herself to sink back into sleep, her thoughts drifted and eddied, disturbing her with splintered pictures—light glinting on a brass poker, the texture of an expensive rug as she lay with her cheek against it, Mark Bourke's strained face bending over her. And Chris—she wouldn't allow herself to think about Chris. Not yet.

A doctor came, examined her, said reassuring things, told her she could now have visitors, and departed on a crest of importance. The nurse who bustled in to plump up her pillows was young and enthusiastic and had not yet acquired the briskly competent air of her more experienced colleagues. "Inspector Ashton," she said, "there was a whole lot about you on the television, risking your life and all that!"

At Carol's frown she added, "Don't you remember it all? People don't often, when they're hit on the head."

"I remember."

Bourke appeared in the doorway. The nurse smiled at him in recognition, commented how he'd been on television too, admonished Carol not to do anything but rest, and left them alone.

"The doctor said you've got a concussion, but nothing broken." Bourke had none of his usual ease with her. He looked and sounded awkward.

It was an effort to talk. "The doctor told me how lucky I am."

"No one's been allowed to see you until now. Sybil's waiting outside. Then, if you feel well enough, you'll be asked for a statement."

She made no reply. He cleared his throat. "Carol we had to do it. She would have killed you."

With a jolt of certainty she knew Mark and his team had shot and killed Chris to save her life. Now he faced a full police inquiry and a public inquest.

"Mark..."

"Don't say anything. It's okay. Everything'll be all right."

She said, "How arrogant of me to think she loved me enough not to hurt me."

He touched her shoulder. "Don't say that. I waited far too long to give the signal to go in. We had enough on her husband's death, but I wanted Fiona Brandstett too."

"Don't blame yourself about me. That's absurd. The recording, have you listened to it?"

He smiled, a little of the old Bourke surfacing. "We're home and hosed, Carol. She incriminates herself comprehensively, in the process giving a good general impression of a psychopath at work. And, as far as your relationship with her is concerned, there's nothing mentioned that could be dangerous."

"Dangerous?" said Carol bitterly. "You mean I can rest easy, secure in the knowledge that my true identity is still not public?"

"Isn't that for the best?"

She thought, Is it so wrong to want to keep my private life and my public life separate? Why should it be an issue I have to face?

Sybil's face was pale and tired. The comfort of her presence filled Carol with a rush of delight. She tried to sit up, subsided with a groan, and said, "Darling, where've you been? I've missed you."

"I've been here all night, just down the hall. I wanted to be with you, but they wouldn't let me in. Then, when the doctor told us you were all right, Mark said he had to see you first." She paused, then said, "He told me everything that happened."

"Mark saved me in more ways than one," said Carol drily.

Sybil looked away. "About Christine—"

"About Christine there's nothing to say—unless you want to comment on my total lack of objectivity."

Hearing the biting note in Carol's voice, Sybil took her hand, interlocking their fingers. "It must be almost impossible to love someone and be objective about her."

"That can't be true. I can be objective about you."

"Oh?"

"You're clearly wonderful."

Sybil's smile warmed the air between them. "Gosh," she said with gentle mockery, "to be so clear sighted *and* to write persuasive letters, too."

"Did I persuade you?"

"Of course you did." She grinned. "But then, I'm awfully suggestible."

Carol said, "Do you love me?"

"Jeffrey I love," said Sybil. Her smile widened. "You—I'm quite keen on."

Bella Books, Inc.

Women. Books. Even Better Together.

P.O. Box 10543
Tallahassee, FL 32302

Phone: 800-729-4992
www.bellabooks.com